by
Samarpan

Tiya

A Parrot's Journey Home

by

Samarpan

HarperCollins *Publishers* India
a joint venture with

New Delhi

First published in India in 2009 by
HarperCollins *Publishers* India
a joint venture with
The India Today Group

Copyright © Samarpan 2009

1 3 5 7 9 8 6 4 2

ISBN: 978-81-7223-832-2

Samarpan asserts the moral right to be identified as the author
of this work.

HarperCollins *Publishers*
A-53, Sector 57, Noida 201301, India
77-85 Fulham Palace Road, London W6 8JB, United Kingdom
Hazelton Lanes, 55 Avenue Road, Suite 2900, Toronto, Ontario M5R 3L2
and 1995 Markham Road, Scarborough, Ontario M1B 5M8, Canada
25 Ryde Road, Pymble, Sydney, NSW 2073, Australia
31 View Road, Glenfield, Auckland 10, New Zealand
10 East 53rd Street, New York NY 10022, USA

Typeset in 11/14 Weiss
InoSoft Systems

Printed and bound at
Thomson Press (India) Ltd.

Contents

Foreword

It is with great pleasure that I introduce the first published work of my good friend Samarpan, a monk. *Tiya – A Parrot's Journey Home* is fresh, attractive, humorous and witty. Not many first books can boast of such virtues.

The central character of the work is Tiya, a parrot who embarks on an adventure that soon turns out to be a series of misadventures. He eventually turns homeward, but his return journey seems to take him farther and farther away from the banyan tree, in which he used to live. In the process – as in all fables – he learns some important things about himself.

Tiya is easy to read because it wears its learning lightly (yet another virtue!). What has been presented through this simple story of a parrot's wanderings, is actually the Vedantic concept of negation, according to which every person has to go through the inessential, before he can outgrow the limitations imposed on him by his nature. Similarly, the use of Hans the swan in the story, reflects that aspect of Yogic philosophy, according to which, Nature takes a person through various experiences – towards freedom from every kind of limitation.

It is wonderful to see Samarpan take time off from his rigorous and strenuous monastic schedule, to write a book for all ages and all seasons. More power to his pen and to his tribe.

Upamanyu Chatterjee
New Delhi

Prologue

You are much more than what you think you are, and you can achieve much more than you are achieving now.

– Tiya

Upon the same tree there are two birds of beautiful plumage, most friendly to each other, one eating the fruits, the other sitting there calm and silent without eating – the one on the lower branch eating sweet and bitter fruits in turn and becoming happy and unhappy, but the other one on the top, calm and majestic; he eats neither sweet nor bitter fruits, cares neither for happiness nor misery, immersed in his own glory.

– Swami Vivekananda

Part I

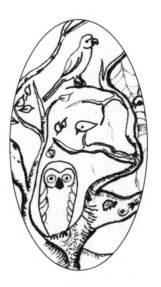

The Banyan

'Good morning good people,' I mumbled, with sleep-laden eyes, to no one in particular. This was a routine morning greeting by me – Tiya-the-parrot-of-the-banyan – to all the other birds of the tree. There was no response – this was also a routine. Being a late riser, I was accustomed to not seeing my fellow-birds on waking up, as they were already out and busy practising 'the early bird'. Unfortunately for me, dawn always made my eyelids heavier and prompted me to sink into a deeper sleep.

Why didn't these feather-balls slow down a bit and enjoy life? Flight – alight – flight. Eat – rest – eat. This is what they called life! If only they knew what it was to feel the warmth of the sun on one's feathers while still in bed, or to feel the wind's soft touch on the face with one's eyes closed, or to simply contemplate on this and that. But no! They had to hurry each morning, as if the banyan was coming to an end any minute.

These musings of mine were also routine. To muse was my nature. Others thought that I contemplated so much because I was lazy. But I was neither a dreamer, nor a lazy bird; it was just that I acted only when I felt it was necessary – and then I acted fast. The rest of my time was devoted to thinking – chattering – thinking. In any case, being a veggie, I did not have to compete much for my livelihood. My limited needs gave me a lot of space – and time.

I yawned, stretched my limbs and wings, preened my green feathers, moved my neck right and left, and was ready to leave the good old banyan for the day. This tree had been my shelter from my pre-memory days, and everyone connected with it, considered it to be old and secure. The animals and birds who lived here had heard from their fathers that the banyan had looked just as old when they were kids. Over the years these tales had led to the firm belief that the tree was unborn and eternal. It was ridiculous, but it conveyed the idea.

The branches of our banyan housed thousands of feathered bipeds; its shade sheltered hundreds of quadrupeds; and its trunk teemed with millions of centi- deci- and millipedes. It had been a silent witness to every kind of personality, along with their hopes and expectations, sweeps to success and downslides into oblivion.

At times I wondered how this wise banyan rated me. Did he consider me adventurous? A bit on the louder side? A bird with a pure heart? Or simply of no consequence? But there was no way to get an answer.

I stopped my musings and pushed my feet against the branch, to launch myself into the air and take on the world. To snatch from the universe whatever I needed for my wants and vanity. This too was a routine.

'Get ready birdies, here comes Tiya!' I hollered and was soon whirling and flying in no particular direction. The world belonged to us, especially to me.

It was like any other day.

'Welcome Tiya, you lazy featherhead. Wasting the brilliant morning away in your stupid laziness! You just missed a good supply of bugs.'

'You should have saved a little for me. After all, what are friends for?' I said good-naturedly.

'Being a true friend, I think of you as myself, so I ate up your share too. Ha, ha, ha!' came the reply.

'Ha, ha to you, old wing! With you around, I would never need an enemy.'

An elderly voice told us off: 'Why can't you two make a little less noise? You are scaring the worms away. Won't you birds ever grow up?'

'Yes dear uncle! We are growing, and with our growth our vocal chords are growing too. I thought you would have appreciated the development, uncle!' I jeered.

'Nuts. And *stop* calling me your uncle. Others will think I belong to the gutter like you!'

I didn't mind the insult. I had branded this bird as a 'fossil' because he thought my progressive ideas were outlandish. It was nothing but plain jealousy. My exuberance was idolised by the young, but condemned by the doddering retired types. Knowing that popularity came for a price, I overlooked some losses and made up for it with adulation from others.

I was busy with this bantering, when I saw Mr Owl return from his night out. He was quite old and was considered to have special powers. We were on affectionate terms, but due to my immaturity, I also took the liberty of teasing him occasionally. Just then the morning light was blinding him, and as he used to say, 'dimming the wits out of him'. He was flying fast to avoid the glare, but was neither fast nor sleepy enough to miss me.

Mr Owl blinked rapidly and changed his course to land softly near me. He looked intently and said, 'Tiya, your life may undergo a great change today. Be careful.' The words were slow, thoughtful and hesitant.

'Forecasting is *our* speciality, dear grandpa! It's parrots who pick the tarot cards and tell people's fortune. Just because I have not been trapped and trained by those cheats, does not mean that you can take away what is rightfully mine. Ha, ha! Even the crows will laugh to death if they hear you.'

Mr Owl never liked to be reminded of his age, although he took full advantage of his senior bird status. Nor did he like irresponsible reactions to his prophecies. Before he hurried away he mumbled something about the futility of opening his beak before fools.

His words, however, had unlocked the vocal gates of the other birds.

'A great change indeed! In a place where nothing changes except the seasons, and perhaps coats of feathers for some of us.'

'Tiya, the wise owl's words have never proved wrong. Who knows? I am a bit nervous.'

'Will you recognise me when you are famous?'

'Tiya, to forget is okay, but to remember is great.'

Birds, and their words! I had to be stern with them, 'Do you know, you all sound like a bunch of belching buffaloes?' I said.

The discussion continued for a while, but when nothing unusual emerged, it veered off to more juicy subjects. With the attention of the other birds diverted, I slipped away. I wanted to visit Mr Woodpecker, who had been my mentor for a long time. His bill was powerful and chisel-like for pecking deep holes in tree trunks. And like his bill, his mind was sharp too. I was very friendly with him and used to listen to the words of wisdom that he uttered between his pecking. I also appreciated the power of his bill, so I preferred never to contradict him. It was his habit to tolerate my words and behaviour with an indulgent smile, but at times, with a sharp warning peck at the wood. But, like every other bird, he was out gathering food somewhere, so I went back to my refuge – the good old banyan tree.

When I reached there, I could see no one around except the insects. They too were busy pushing and carrying things in every direction. Occasionally a honeybee was returning from its usual round of errands. Mr Owl was asleep and snoring.

I alighted on my branch and became aware of an invisible and overwhelming presence landing near me. The banyan seemed to shudder.

There was no reason for alarm. The banyan was like a magician's cellar where one often encountered the bizarre. The unexpected was what one expected, and the abnormal appeared quite normal here. I'll narrate a few experiences of mine, to explain.

I had first become conscious of my existence a long time ago on this very tree. My first memory is of the heavy burden of my body, which was making me feel oppressed and miserable. I wanted to get rid of it, but was attacked by another problem in the form of hunger, which seemed much more threatening. It was only with maturity in later months, when I realised that the external and the internal problem were one and the same.

The body created hunger, and eating created the body. Thus the wheel rolled on. What a situation to be in! No wonder the folks of this banyan were banana-brained.

I tottered foolishly towards Mr Dove for help, who said, 'Don't worry about problems. They come and go. You alone are permanent here. You are – and you will be. Concentrate on what you have without worrying about what you do not have. That is the way to happiness.'

That was my first brush with existence and philosophy. I remember how I cursed both and wished that they did not exist. Here I was miserable with hunger, and instead of getting seeds, I was being fed with sermons. Some years later, I had tried starting an anti-philosophy forum, but unfortunately, like many of my other mega plans, it did not kick-start.

Mr Dove claimed to be a philosopher and offered theories and suggestions for everything. Most of them contradicted each other, but he never accepted that fact. It was common to find him muttering to himself, 'A bird is not understood in his own tree.' The birds laughed at him for all that he said and did, but they also went to him for counsel during a crisis. But Mr Dove was Mr

Dove. Once he advised a hummingbird to grow a moustache to look important. When the bird asked him how to do it, he commented, 'I am not God, only a consultant.'

While seeking the answers to my problems, I had had another encounter with a dashing young cuckoo whom I idolised along with many other young birds. The elders hated him for reasons that were not clear to us then. They considered him a bad influence and we were advised to stay clear of him. But we followed him wherever he went. The dark-complexioned bird had a charming personality, a divine voice, a gift for magical words and a majestic gait. He was also the leader of the 'Bird Liberation Forum'. No one knew what exactly this forum was meant to do, but the younger generation was all for it, and tried to ape the songs composed by Mr Cuckoo.

As on many other days, I was very hungry that day, and food was suddenly scarce. I was very young and did not know much about the ways of the world. I needed liberation from these inner and outer limitations, and so I believed that my problem was fit to be addressed before the forum. I presented my case before Mr Cuckoo as best as I could, but even before I could complete it, he burst out laughing and commanded me in a grave voice: 'You the young and mighty. The wide world awaits your arrival. Go! Cheat, steal or loot. This is the secret of survival. You have nothing to lose but your hunger.' He then curtly asked me to remove myself from his presence.

It was much later that I came to know about the darker side of his life – absolutely *uninspiring*. The 'Forum of Liberation' was meant only for his own liberation from looking after his offspring!

The banyan was as weird a place as it could be. So naturally I was not worried when I felt an invisible presence.

That is when I distinctly heard a formless voice saying: 'You are no ordinary parrot.'

These unusual words, coming from nowhere in particular, brought me back to the present. I looked around to see the speaker and his possible audience, but only an absence met my eyes. It was quite disturbing – alarming, in fact. We birds believe more in speaking than listening. To us, speech means power, and listening means loss of power. In this case, not only was I the listener, but I was not even able to see the speaker. *Scary*.

There was no one around, so the words that I had just heard were definitely just for me. This created crosscurrents in my mind. I had my share of qualities that made me feel good at times – and also made me a bit different from others, particularly the crows. But this did not mean that I was extraordinary. All of us are shaped by our experiences and understanding of them. Today, while narrating this story, I know myself as Tiya the parrot – and also much more than that. But in those green days of mine, I knew myself as Tiya, a-parrot-of-the-banyan – a bird of no special consequence. Thus the words of the unseen speaker were difficult to digest.

Also, on hearing those five words being uttered, a dormant desire for recognition suddenly awoke within me. One always feels puffed up when praised – more so, when the praise is misplaced. The mental turbulence caused by flattering words bloats the personality beyond proportion. It was the same with me. I felt important and turned my head around with a grave air. I might even have nodded.

On the other hand, I felt disturbed because I was an active member of 'The Brotherhood of Birds' that was founded on the motto, 'all birds are equal', Some birds who were more successful, had tried to add the clause 'some are more equal than others', but they had been hooted out. How could I then accept myself as an extraordinary bird when I had sworn to be one of the crowd? I had always felt that the future of the banyan, and its birds, depended a lot upon me. It was based on these principles that I had been living my life.

Hope, expectation, excitement and apprehension were driving me crazy. I felt like saying something to ease the situation, but was stopped by my ego that had always veered on the sensitive side. The mental duel that ensued between my ego and myself, sounded something like this:

> Let me speak to this voice.
> *Mind your own business.*
> That is what I wish to do.
> *You better ignore him.*
> Ignoring leads to ignorance.
> *Ignorance is bliss. Be firm.*
> My will power has always been leaky.
> *Persuade yourself not to speak.*
> Persuading others is easy.
> *You are a disgusting fool.*

I inhaled deeply and decided to make a frontal attack on this Mr Voice. Answering him was easy. I had nothing to hide – whereas he was hiding. To me it was a sure sign of his weakness. Those were the days when I was most vocal about things I knew the least. This characteristic of mine had earned me victories in every argument. One often tends to be the most assertive when one knows the least. The listeners who know the truth ignore you, whereas those who do not, feel awed by your confidence and assertiveness. In either case, you have the satisfaction of silencing your opponents. That is why I had stuck to the theory that 'life is all about assertion', and also, 'he who shouts, survives'.

The voice had no form, so I looked in no particular direction and said, 'I don't know who you are. Nor do I know the reason behind your disturbing ideas about me. I also have no inkling of what you want from me. But could you please explain why your voice is present and your body absent?'

'Hmm. Clever, aren't you? The likes of you are not made everyday.'

Was it a compliment? I was not sure. On the saving side, at least it was now clear that the words were meant for me. My excitement mounted at the thought that I really was extraordinary. I could feel myself growing in size, as well as outgrowing my principles. Everyone in this world wants to forget about feeling ordinary. So, when one is thought to be more than ordinary, why should one abide by rules and promises?

I had nothing to say, and Mr Voice continued, 'You know Tiya . . . you do not belong to this place.'

Lightning in a blue sky would have startled me less. How did he know my name? Was he a magician? Or the ghost of one of Mr Owl's ancestors?

My claws sank deeper into the branch on which I was sitting.

A silence followed between us both. The absence of words was now more overpowering than their presence had been. I waited long. The ninth hell must be something like this – a great wait in the burning desert for the unknown to happen.

I wanted to ask Mr Voice many questions, but felt feeble and tiny under the pressure of an unseen power. In a strained voice, I somehow blurted out, 'Who are you, sir?'

There was no reply. I only felt a sense of increasing power around me, and the loss of my own power in consequence. My natural exuberance had vanished; I was not able to think clearly, leave alone appear natural!

Natural – that is what describes my personality perfectly. I am who I am, and act as I am. I think I stood out, even in those early days, because of this single factor, and the birds of the banyan thought me unnatural simply because I was not. You may then wonder why I was here? Well, this story is about that.

I made another feeble attempt, 'Who are you, sir?'

'What is there in a name?' asked back the voice.

Now that the spell was broken, my tone was normal again.

'What about your form, sir?'

'What is there in a form?'

'What do you want from me, sir?'

'What is there in action?'

'What brings you here, sir?'

'What is there in a goal?'

'Where are you from, sir?'

Judging by the trend of the answers, it was a useless question.

'Home is where I am.'

Here I was – proud of my melodious name – Tiya; proud of my plumage, my species, my banyan tree, my skills and my thinking. And there he was – nameless, formless, actionless, goalless and homeless! How dare he blast away my greatness, my ideas, my opinions and my philosophy?

I kept silent. Although, as a bird, I was never in favour of silence, I had always felt that it was a good way to protect oneself in a tight situation. It was definitely helpful when you did not want to tell someone powerful what you really thought of him, on his face. However, emotions do not require the medium of words. Mr Voice must have felt my annoyance, for he suddenly said, 'Call me Hans, if you like. I am not fussy about a petty thing like a name.' I remained silent, and he continued, 'Tiya, you are much more than what you think you are, and you can achieve much more than what you think you can. You need to realise this through experience, for which you have to get out of this place.'

Holy Feathers! This voice belonged to a lunatic asylum, I thought to myself, and said, 'Sir, all birds are equal, and every one is great. We even have a movement aimed towards that. I am glad to mention that I am its proud member.'

'You should be congratulated on your achievements, no doubt! But, if you want to quit this tomfoolery and try to understand things, you should know that there are more real matters in this world than idle ideals. The time has not yet come for all birds to understand and practise their equality, nor has the time come for them to go to the moon. On the other hand, *your* time has come; just don't ask me how or why!'

Time for what? The fellow was a split open jackfruit. Anyway, since his words seemed encouraging and positive, I said nothing. I also felt happy because I hadn't abandoned the principle of equality of all birds in any way. But, to leave the banyan! That was something difficult for me to conceive.

'Sir, can't I achieve everything here on this banyan?'

'The banyan is not the end of the world, but just the beginning. One day you will realise that there is much more to life than this tree. You start once, and the rest will follow on its own. You will see things, experience them, and learn from them. These experiences will be bitter at times, and at other times sweet, but you will have to move on; holding on to any one experience will limit you. Whenever in doubt, you will hear my voice. Think of me as your guide and benefactor. I advise you to listen to what I say, otherwise . . .'

'Otherwise what?' I did not allow him to complete the sentence. My parrot ego was now wide-awake and it made my words sound as menacing as cold steel.

'You will sink farther down.'

'Down is not far below,' I said, wanting to be funny. To add punch, I looked down the tree.

'You think so, silly parrot? You have swallowed a lot of words without knowing what they mean, and you use them without understanding. Anger is not a sign of intelligence. You will realise this soon.'

The ring of warning in his tone was menacing. So, I thought it better to be voiceless before the formless. He continued, 'You need to know that you are different; you need to realise that you are much more than what you think you are; and you need to actualise this through your actions, by achieving more than you think you can. In a word, you have to find yourself. As I said, I am here to guide and protect you through words. If you ever want to see me desperately, I will appear before you in the form of a swan. But if you see my real form, you may swoon.'

See a swan and swoon. Ha! He had a sense of humour. Every year we used to see swans crossing our land, without ever taking a break at our banyan tree. They were graceful and majestic, but we were unanimous in thinking of them as snobs, since they never landed near us. This Mr Hans, despite the respect he aroused in me, seemed extra proud.

How wrong I was then!

I was curious to see Mr Hans, but not terribly eager. So, nothing happened.

As surprising as his appearance had been, I suddenly felt him gone, and this made me feel lonely. I wanted his company for a little longer, but now the outside emptiness balanced the emptiness within me.

The words of Hans were too powerful to ignore, so without considering the consequences, or waiting for my friends to return, I flew away from the banyan – towards the unknown – through the unknown – in search of the unknown.

The wise owl had indeed been correct.

Part JJ

Adventures

The Playground

Directed by my past, propelled by my present and pulled by my future, I flew in search of finding the unknown. Enthusiasm, curiosity and hope gave me company. I didn't know whether I was running away from something, or moving towards it. I didn't even know where I was headed – my body was just following my head and my wings were beating automatically. My only thought at that time was, that I had to do what Mr Hans had told me – to realise that I was much more than what met the eyes.

Even then, an occasional doubt would raise its head and I would struggle to calm myself:

Where are you going birdie? The banyan has been good enough for you. Why do you want to fly from security to insecurity?

Keep quiet and fly. Do what Hans has asked you to do. You have spent your whole life following your own ego. Follow someone superior to you, for once.

Aren't you like a kid groping in the darkness for the jar of cookies that has already been removed by a careful mom? And how do you know that Mr Hans is not mad like Mr Dove?

Maybe, but let me discover it the hard way.

You might be chasing a lie.

It is better than chasing birds.

You won't get a thing.

Even otherwise I wasn't getting much.

My flight continued despite such speed-breakers. Soon I was far away from the landscape that was familiar to me. I had no one whom I could call my own, so the whole world was mine. It was now easy for me to make friends, experiment, explore and experience – the ideal way to educate oneself.

From the low height at which I was flying, I saw a huge field where a large number of children were excitedly playing a game of football. Many grown-ups were watching from a distance, without interfering. I too alighted on a tree and watched. As I understood, the ball was not to be touched with the hands during the game. There was great enthusiasm all around, when a sudden commotion broke out.

'Foul! Foul!'

'Why is it a foul?'

'Because from this moment onwards, touching the ball with one's legs has become a foul. You can only use your hands. So now, give us a free throw against you.'

'What do you mean? Who gave you the authority to change the rule?'

'Look, man! You may leave if you don't agree with our rules. What is the fun in playing with the same rules forever? If you have to play with us, you have to listen to what we say.'

'This is unfair!'

'What is unfair? We keep changing the rules whenever it suits us.'

'But why not find a simpler rule to decide the winner? Since the rules get changed, we can change it once more.'

'And, what might that be?'

'We can fight it out with our hands. The winner will take all.'

The fight broke out faster than it had taken me to understand the situation. Hands were now used freely, and instead of the ball, the target was the opponents' bodies.

'That is a foul!'

'What is a foul?'

'Why did you use your legs, and why did you spit?'

'It is a free fight, you papaya. Here's another juicy one!'

Where had I reached? We banyan birds were extremely particular about rules and discipline. Norms were not changed every minute. Even the crow couples maintained their code of friendship and fighting. Where had I landed? Why were the elders not coming forward to intervene? Whenever a fight broke out at the banyan, the wiser birds mediated. May be the grown-ups of this place were not really grown-ups. Or, may be they had also been brought up in this way, so they thought it was normal. They probably thought that to be successful, one had to adjust successfully.

Much later, during my many adventures, I was to realise that indeed the rules of the game kept changing forever. One had to adjust to the whims of the powerful. But it was always me who had to adjust with them or get crushed. Worse still, I had to fly from place to place to save my feathers. But more of that later.

I was about to get out of the place, when someone spotted me.

'Look at that tail! Stop the game. Come, let us catch the beaky and get a feather each as a prize.'

The crowd was galvanised into one. Even the grown-ups joined in. It was unbelievable to see their unity, in contrast to the divisiveness that I had just seen. When it came to harming others, they had fixed rules! Missiles flew at me from every direction.

Not being a high flier, I had to look for an escape route, but the voices kept chasing me.

'Greeno! Grant us a gift of your feathers. Be sporting.'

The chants of these boisterous kids terrified me – much more than Mr Eagle's ever had.

'Let us get a net and catch him. He appears smart. We could teach him to cheer us during our games.'

'The bird has no spirit – he should have joined us on his own.'

'Bitter or sweet, let's taste the parakeet!'

They had no rules – they could do anything. So there was nothing for me to think about, I could only act. With the net coming from above and spreading all around, my escape routes were closing.

I tried to trick them by diving to the ground and lying still, so that they thought I was tired and had given up all hopes of escape. Shouts of 'Got him finally!' now echoed from all directions.

I kept my eyes closed, and when I felt that the crowd was concentrating on coming closer, I shot up into the sky. The net had been removed – no rules, you know.

'Get him, get him, the trickster!' The shouts, accompanied by stones, chased me for a while, and one stone narrowly missed me. But I was out and safe.

I flew for my life – completely directionless.

The Fags

What a dangerous way to start a new life. I felt sad – more so because I did not know where I had gone wrong. If this first encounter was a taste of things to come, then life was going to be really difficult. But what option had I other than flying? Behind me were the riotous kids who followed no rules, and ahead of me was uncertainty. So, I flew on.

A high mountain appeared in the horizon. I had never seen anything as huge as this. I could not fly around it, nor could I cross over it. My wings were too delicate for such a difficult task. Unlike many other powerful birds, parrots are not made for high and strenuous flying.

As I flew closer, I saw a tiny gap in the mountain face. It was *so* narrow that I had to squeeze hard to pass through it. In the process, I bruised myself. I still wonder how I overcame my fear and plunged into this dark, narrow crack. It was a risk that only someone stupid or insane might take. Probably I was both.

A whole new world opened up before me as I emerged out of the crevice. But, if I had known what awaited me on the other side, I would have never entered the gap; nor would there have been this unusual story for me to tell.

I had reached the land of beauty. In fact, the land of perfect beauty. Any more of it would have been meaningless; and any less, would not have diminished from its splendour. It was poetry in three-dimension. I suddenly became conscious of myself and felt ashamed of the old banyan tree where I had lived since my birth. I also felt that I didn't belong to this place.

Strands of music wafted lazily in the air. Even the leaves and the flowers seemed to breathe melodies, and the atmosphere appeared to vibrate with the soft ringing of bells. The peals of laughter gliding here and there seemed to emanate from people who had never faced any sorrow in life. We birds are famous for our voices, which range over a variety of sounds, from cawing and shrieking, to cooing, trilling and twittering. But what was coming to my ears was far beyond my experience. I felt fresh, relaxed and full of energy.

I had fallen into a doze when I heard footsteps approaching – steps that sounded softer than rose petals falling on the soft green grass. A beautiful presence, probably someone who was a resident of that place, approached me.

I lost my voice in the presence of this radiant being.

With a smile it came closer, and asked me who I was. I suddenly felt at ease, and overcoming my nervousness introduced myself as Tiya, a parrot. In turn, this being introduced itself as a Fay.

I dared to ask, 'Sir, what land is this? Are you the king of this place?'

'No dear, I am not the king. Nor is anybody else. We are all equals here. This land is known as the land of the Fays.' The sweetness in his voice was so intoxicating that I nearly fell asleep.

If there was a place where one could live forever, this was it. One lifetime would have been too brief to drink in the beauty of the land.

Hesitatingly I asked if I could stay there, to which Monsieur Fay gladly agreed. He added that there were no restrictions in joining the Fays – in fact not many beings came to live here. I wondered why? I also felt sorry for the rest of the world – they did not know what they were missing.

Unlike our banyan, this land was not crowded. The tree on which I now made my home, gave me an excellent view of the entire place. From my spot, I could see the Fays move about in the distance, singing and cooing softly. 'Mr Cuckoo! Where are you? Come, listen to the singing. Come, hear what is real melody,' I couldn't help muttering to myself.

To my untrained eyes, all the Fays looked alike. I was once told that human beings were not able to distinguish one parrot from the other. How I had laughed then! I now wondered what the Fays would think of me. But I felt they were so gentle that they would not laugh and embarrass me.

The desire to be friendly with other Fays never crossed my mind; I was happy with my M Fay who regularly visited me. His coming and going, and his presence and absence, kept me intoxicated.

In an attempt to improve my personality, I decided to learn singing and dancing. M Fay readily agreed to be my tutor, which made me feel as if the floodgates of divine happiness had opened up. Now my daily routine consisted of talking and taking lessons. It was paradise.

Despite having a great teacher, I proved to be a failure as a pupil. Instead of musical notes, only squawks escaped my throat, and whenever I tried to impress him, I could only cut a sorry figure. The harder I tried, the worse my performance became. I kept cursing my maker and my destiny, for having given me a voice and a body that was fit for nothing. To compensate for my inability to learn, I engaged in foolish and undignified acts to please M Fay. When I look back on those days, I don't blame him for my misadventures. Whatever I had done was of my own doing, and of my own choice.

My life continued like this – I do not know for how long. Maybe it wasn't for many days, but I was too intoxicated to keep count.

The bubble pricked one day when I noticed a web of scratches and fine scars all over M Fay's body. Why had I been blind to this before? My head reeled and I failed to restrain myself.

'What has happened to you, M Fay? How did you get scratches all over your beautiful body? You look terrible,' I blurted out.

My friend responded with an amused smile. That smile! I could have spent my whole life watching it! But M Fay brought me back to reality by drawing my attention to his fingers with a glance.

Holy feathers! How had I missed such a sight? All of M Fay's fingers, and in fact that of every Fay, tapered into razor-sharp tips! A faint scream must have escaped me. Such beauty everywhere, and all of it ending in deathly sharpness. It was a wonder that these creatures survived each other. 'Bravo Creator! What a mess you have created,' I thought as I panted in fear.

The churning whirlpool of my thoughts was stopped by M Fay's melodious voice. 'Why do you look surprised, dear? Stroking and petting is in our nature, we love each other so much. And that is when the sharp edges of our fingers scratch and cut. But, we cannot blame them. The good Lord has made us thus.'

It is still a mystery to me why anyone would do something that ended in pain. May be it is in their nature. Or may be it is just ignorance. But in those days, I was green and I unjustly thought that the Fays were rather stupid. So I decided to enlighten M Fay.

Sermons are normally resented, and more so, if the receiving party is guilty. However, M Fay's gentleness gave me courage to speak out. 'Why don't you maintain a minimum distance, you silly people? Don't you feel the pain?' I demanded.

In the past, my tone would have been much rougher, but partly due to the new land, and partly because of M Fay, my words were coming out softer than I had intended. 'Obviously we feel the pain, my dear. But why does your voice sound a little on the higher side? I think, I even heard you scream. Don't you like me anymore?'

I ignored his words and continued with my unsuccessful attempts at reform.

'You are so dumb. Why don't you stop petting and stroking? That will save you from all the cuts and scars.'

'We are loving by nature, my sugar candy. We have been created this way. Body and mind – it is a package. Our goal is to love and be loved, my dear friend.'

His voice and words were seductive. But, I made one last attempt at harshness.

'Even at the cost of your own pain . . . you are hare-brained!'

'We cannot and must not stop loving each other. Why worry about the result when you are able to do what you want to do, and also what you are destined to do, dear? In any case, our love compensates for the pain caused by our fingers. What is there in life other than attaining pleasure and happiness? If we have to suffer a bit to get it, where is the harm in that? And, another thing – your harsh words are so unsuited to your good nature. Why, they may even dry up the flowers around. Allow me to soothe your throat.'

This place had a magic about it that put me in a kind of trance. Before I could react or understand what M Fay intended to do, he caressed me round my neck, as if putting my voice to sleep. I couldn't talk and I seemed drugged into silence.

M Fay continued, 'Allow me to leave, my feathered beauty. I do wish to be with you a little longer, but I am busy today and have to complete my share of love. The daily round of getting and giving, you know. Now that you are one of us, I shall ask my friends to put your name on their list of rounds.'

With a sweet glance M Fay made a move to leave. And then the spell broke.

What did he mean by my being one of them? Why did he want others to visit me, when they had never done so before? For reasons unknown to me, my brain started working again, and I became conscious of myself.

That is when I felt the red ring of blood around my tender green neck. The touch of that scheming Fay! It had had the effect of a razor on my throat. Plague of the land! Now I would have to carry this red ring on my neck all my life. This was what they called love and friendship!

My anger was not as fiery as in the past, but for this place, it was an inferno. 'Silly ass. Horse thief. Never come near me. You and your gang of looter friends! You won't get me ever again. You and your beauty! May you all drown in a pool of cow dung. May you slip and fall into an ocean of sewage. May you . . . may you . . .'

'Dear, dear. Calm down.'

'How can I calm down? You and your beauty – and your voice and good manners – your land and your philosophy. May black ink rain on your leaky roofs. May green water flood your fields. May scum grow on your bodies. May . . . may . . .'

'Dear, I love you. I care for you. Have you forgotten our moments spent together?'

'Even I love you and care for you. Only my fingers are not as sharp as yours, so I cannot show my love in that way. Take your love and dump it in the nearest ditch.'

'You will go away, isn't it? Like the many others. But, remember that I will always be waiting for you. You are so special.'

'Yes, special indeed. Easy to butcher.'

I was angry beyond measure. But what does a red rag do to a bull? And here I was with a permanent red ring before my eyes. There was no way for me to calm down now. In my fuming rage I had not noticed that my fingernails had started growing, and getting sharper. The magic in the touch of the Fays would make me just like them. In no time I would have the body, brain and emotions of these creatures. If I had to survive and save my individuality, I had to dash out of the place. Nothing could hold me back now.

I gave a shake to my feathers, and with a strong kick and a flap of my wings, I was airborne. Good riddance to these imbeciles. Playing with the lives of innocents! I wish they scratched out the beauty from their own bodies, rather than scratching others to death. Killing others in the name of love and friendship was their favourite pastime.

I still carry the red ring round my neck as the mark of my visit to the land of the Fays. Every

time you see a green parrot with a red ring, you
will know where it has been.

The Zarys

My days spent with the Fays had proved to be a
meaningless waste. I had conjured up many dreams
for myself, and they had ended cruelly. The
pleasing music of my expectations had exploded
into the reality of almost getting butchered. I was
angry, very angry.

But anger gave me energy. As I flew, the air
moaned under my body, and past the sides of my
wings. I was flying and talking to myself at the
same speed. The emerging words clustered round
my head like dancers with spears in their hands
circling a blazing fire – harmless but frightening.
The dialogue went something like this:

You are a fool. How could you conclude that
beauty means goodness and stability? You had
experienced its darker side with Mr Cuckoo, and
Mr Woodpecker had told you that what appears
good to you, may not necessarily be good for you.
You have been hit badly so many times in the past.
But, you don't seem to learn.

One always hopes that each experience will be different from the previous one; and one survives on the belief that this time one won't get hit.

Now you must carry the red ring of your failed hopes round your neck.

I wish I had scratched M Fay's face.

Wisdom always comes after the event.

I agree. I am full of anger with the Fays, with beauty, with the world, and with my fate. I am angry even with myself. I feel cheated.

Forget the Fays as a bad dream. If you are feeling cheated, then know that you are equally responsible for it. Your desires and hopes provided the fuel; M Fay only supplied the spark. Now cool down.

I will . . . provided I can skin a lion alive, kick an elephant away with my foot, and uproot a tree with my mere breath. I feel like doing these things and much more . . .

I saw an elephant at a distance and in my blind rage I flew towards it to give it a kick. On seeing me approach, it raised its powerful trunk in anticipation of an attack. I was surprised to see that it had read my intentions. Probably everyone coming out of the land of the Fays tried to take out their anger on this poor creature. I changed my course.

Mr Hans! The brainwashing machine! Mental-poison-delivery-unit! Why did he make me believe that I was unusual? Why had he pushed me into this mess? What did he want from me? My disembodiment to make me a mere voice like him? Today, I regret that I had ever had such thoughts. But anger makes one nasty; as you must know.

Despite my rage, I flew on, and soon I reached a garden. I landed with a thud on the branch of a big tree, expecting it to get shattered, its branches to crack and its leaves to get scorched. But nothing happened and I felt dejected.

I noticed that my wing tips had stopped bleeding and growing sharp. The large garden where I had landed looked old and forgotten, and was full of statues. This land must have flourished in the past, as was evident from so many grand statues. If I was not wary of beauty by now, I might have even thought them to be beautiful. But beauty frightened me, so I did not pay any attention to it. These were just what they were – statues.

Perching on the branch, I dozed off, when suddenly I heard a statue spit furiously, '*Aaaak, thoooo!*'

How could a statue spit? I must have been dreaming. To make sure, I looked around me to check. Holy feathers! These statues were indeed spitting furiously at each other. What I was seeing was not a dream, but extremely real.

What was happening with me? Formless voices, razor-fingered enticers, and now, spitting statues. What was I going to see next – a dancing tree?

I looked carefully at the unbelievable sight! The statues were actually living beings from the waist and above, but frozen rigid from their lower half. They looked like kids playing 'statue' – the difference here being that it was not a game but real life; it was not an option, but rather a compulsion.

What I could make out from the situation was that a statue had spat at me, but somehow missed and hit another. That one in turn spat back at him, but missed . . . and after that the spitting continued with more and more gusto, covering a wider and wider range, with more forceful throws that were less accurate – every next throw acting like a punch for a pinch.

I wondered at the fate of these creatures. What had made them like this? Didn't they want to be free and mobile like everybody else? Could I help them in any way?

'What brings you here, you two-legged nosey feather-fluff?' said someone. 'Don't you have a hole to hide? You green parasite, why have you invaded our land? Get lost this instant!' And with this, he spat at me.

The missile missed again. Like many, they seemed good at talk but bad at work. However, the spit had hit another creature and the place was once again a medley of shots and shouts. Had there been a prize for the best shout and worst throw, no one would have won. All were equally good.

My sympathies had evaporated. The traces of anger from my previous adventure strained to come out in full. My feathers twitched and my chest heaved. Anger blew me up like a balloon. I was a free bird – free to perch, observe or sermonise.

'Parasite yourself! You chunk of stone. Doing nothing but sitting tight and spitting the whole day. It's good that you are rooted to the spot, otherwise the world would have been a worse place. Granite brains!' I had to vent my emotions so that I was not charred by my own anger.

The reaction of the Zarys was instantaneous and furious. All mouths were now directed towards me, and all shots were only for me. It must have

been a long time since they had found a common target. Even before I could react, I noticed the growing stiffness of the statues. Their physical immobility seemed to be increasing in proportion to their verbal abuse. We birds are not really bird-brained as you may think. This was one of those occasions when I put my mind to work – spite was equal to spit and stupefy. I figured that the Zarys only needed to get angry to become solidified. It was quite terrifying – now I understood why Hans had cautioned me not to get angry.

To my horror, I realised that I was also too late; my own feet had petrified into a block of stone! It was the result of my anger. Holy feathers! Where had I landed?

I trembled, panted and sweated. This was the end of my adventures. As always, in such moments of crisis, the good old banyan tree floated in front of my eyes.

'Tiya, smile. Give up your anger and smile. Now!'

It was the voice of Mr Hans. I could not see him, but I could feel his presence. Although I was panic-stricken, I became calmer on hearing his voice. Just the idea of his unseen presence soothed me and his advice saved me from being further stiffened. I calmed myself down by smiling more and more. The smile was less for the Zarys, and more for myself.

Isn't it interesting how certain events that endanger one's life at a point of time, can come as a saving grace at other times? I suddenly felt grateful to the Fays. The sweetness learnt from them was now helping me come out of the dangerous situation in which I had landed. Exigency can make one do unbelievable things. I was now sweetness incarnate. Even my old friend, M Fay could have learnt a few lessons from me. I addressed the nearest of the Zarys, 'Mister, why do you get angry when you know that it turns you into stone? Give up your curses, abuses and spitting, and be free. Learn to love all. In that lies your freedom.'

I was genuine about my intentions, so my words freed me. But the Zarys, for whom they were meant, continued to be unaffected.

'Go preen your feathers, you silly word-repeater! Do you think only you know the art of survival? I know it too. But I must teach a good lesson to all these good-for-nothings even at the cost of my own welfare. I sacrifice my own interests so that others may stay corrected.'

I could not see any correction anywhere around him. Only solidification.

My own de-solidification was complete, but to make sure, I added, 'Sir, not much good seems to have happened here with your anger. I sincerely wish to be of some service to this land. I would feel blessed even if I could free one of you.'

'Get going, you worm-eater! Go land in a volcano!' He was so angry that he could only spit at me with great difficulty. The shot missed and hit another Zary.

I laughed aloud heartily to aid my flight. I am not sure how my laughter might have sounded to others – probably theatrical.

The Revolutionary Birds

There is nothing like fear to galvanise you into action. I was flying away fast from this mad, mad world of the Fays and Zarys. But I continued to tremble from the aftershocks of what I had experienced.

Long ago, before my kismat had lured me to these lands, I had eaten too many nuts one evening. I started dreaming wildly at night. In one of the more frightening dreams, I found myself shedding my feathers and becoming a human. The adventures that followed had left me panting. I was so frightened at the prospect of eating with knives and forks that my sleep – the net that catches dreams – snapped. I woke up to find myself trembling and sweating all over. Although I was relieved that I was not going to be a walking biped, my trembling continued for a while. I moved around the place with a foolish grin on my face for a large part of the next morning.

I felt something like that after I escaped from the land of the Zarys. This is life, I thought – meaningless, but scary. If you did anything, then you rushed towards destruction; if you did nothing, then you waited for destruction to come and meet you. What a funny way to reach the end of one's glory. I would have either been sliced into half, or moulded into a solid block – equally dangerous either ways.

'Getting wiser? I was worried for your safety.' It was Hans the unseen – the voice.

I felt like embracing him and kicking him at the same time. Relief, anger, hurt, joy – a cocktail of emotions surged through me. But I stayed silent.

'Yes, Tiya. This is life. If you take it lightly, you remain a dud; if you take it too seriously, you are doomed.'

'Can't you save something for the others?' I asked weakly.

'Why do you say that? I also saved *you* from becoming history.'

'Yes, but who pushed me there in the first place? You first push, and then pull, to become glorified as my saviour!'

'Tch . . . tch. Don't be piqued, Tiya. Everyone goes through these experiences.'

I was in no mood for his sympathy.

'I wonder if you lost your body in one of these lands. How often have you visited these freaks?'

'No one is a freak, Tiya. We encounter what we create, and we create what we want. No experience is a waste in life.'

Hans' words glided over my head. I wanted to ask him how to go back to my banyan, but before I could say anything, his presence vanished like the summer dew.

My short encounter with Hans, and some energetic flying after that, had changed my earlier mood. In fact I was quite happy to reach a new place, which incidentally, was full of birds. The same species as mine, you know – not creatures or statues. Expressing emotions towards aliens is not my speciality. It's better to live and die, love and quarrel with your own.

I parked myself on a tree. Below me spread a carpet of birds of different sizes, shapes, colours and feathers. They were all engaged in various activities, like picking up things, cracking nuts, catching worms, making heaps of food, cleaning the ground, and so on.

After some time, I was surprised to realise that none of them was airborne – they were only hopping or walking. The birds had perfect feathers on powerful wings, but they were not flying. I wondered why they were behaving like this. Interestingly, they all seemed quite happy the way they were, and some of these disgrace-on-birds were even trying to look important despite their strangeness.

I shouted to one of them and asked what place this was, and why they were walking like animals rather than flying like birds.

'Walking is better than flying, that is our philosophy,' said the bird to me in reply. 'We feel that only the undignified expose their underbelly to commoners. Without meaning to be impolite,

I must add that we were just discussing your lack of decency. You look good, but you are not well bred. Why must you show what you have? The good Lord has given you wings to cover yourself up.'

This was news to me. I had never thought of things this way, nor could I digest it. I argued, 'But, that is what we birds are supposed to do: fly. In that alone lies our freedom and our true nature. Isn't it?'

'Yes, yes. But one must not forget one's dignity. Do you realise that all alpha beings like lions and humans walk, and don't fly? Do you realise that you are born on solid ground, and you die on solid ground? Then, why try to lead your life in the air?'

My head reeled. Where did they get such ideas? They all seemed to be clones of Mr Dove from my good old banyan tree. The bird continued, 'We are trying to bring about a new kind of revolution in which birds will learn the true meaning of dignity, culture and values. This will bring meaning to every bird's life.'

'Did you learn all this in your dreams?' I asked.

'Don't try to be funny,' the bird replied. 'We follow what we have learnt since our birth – not to fly, but walk. We obey this and are happy. Our leader is a wonderful bird. He is respectfully addressed as the "Big Bird" – bless his soul. We listen to what he says. His instructions are not really his own, but he has learnt them from his parents, who learnt from their parents . . . an unbroken tradition of generations, you know. It is all sacred and secret.'

My head reeled, and I was speechless. I could not take anymore. But the bird continued, 'We listen to the sacred commands of the Big Bird. In him lies our ultimate good and immediate gain. He is one of our own and is very caring – and we are overwhelmed with gratitude for this; he has so much on his mind. Normally the Big Bird does not get angry with us, but his anger can uproot a tree if he so desires. All of us are afraid of his anger. It is his express command that we don't fly. We are so obedient that we don't even *think* of flying.'

'But, why do you listen to him or his silly commands when you can be free and independent? Don't you have a mind of your own?'

'Mind your language, sir. His commands are not silly, and you have no right to question us. In any case, I do not know, and do not care if his words are right or wrong. The Big Bird is wise

enough to know our good. We work, he thinks
– division of labour. Do you understand?'

Even before I had the time to reply, a look of
terror came upon his face and he was rooted to
the spot. It was the Big Bird himself. I could make
out from the gait, confidence and air of majesty
that it was him.

'You oaf! Who are you? Why are you up on
the branch? How did you reach there in the first
place?' The powerful voice made me drop down
from the tree like a rotten fruit. His loud question
had hit me in full force.

'I asked you something, you dunce! Who are you?'

His voice cut me like cold steel. I felt afraid
and reduced in size, with my wings powerless,
throat parched, body limp, and mind and senses
numbed. Only my legs seemed alive. And that
too barely – they were trembling too much to be
called alive.

'My name is Tiya sir I am a parrot sir I was
just passing by sir I am sorry sir.' My words got
telescoped in sheer fright.

'Stop it. Enough! Get down to work, you
hollow drum. Words, words, words. One more
word and . . .'

Silence is always more deadly than speech.
Why was he behaving like Mr Eagle with his prey?

Dominating and tormenting, without any reason. And why did I have to listen to him? I felt helpless and quaked with fear.

Now I was face-to-face with him. Unlike his words, he looked innocent and harmless. If he could kill with his words, he could give life with his looks. Earlier, I did not know what I know now: the dangerous ones rarely look dangerous; it is the innocent-looking ones who can be lethal. I had experienced the lethal aspect of innocence in the land of beauty too. But how could one bird behave like this with another? It was unbelievable! He seemed to fire words that exploded like bombs and the very raising of his eyebrows filled one with dread. Something in him made every bird hurry to obey and please him.

Despite my unwillingness, I joined the other birds and began learning how to obey the laws of the land. My obedience was partly due to fear, and partly due to my concern for the birds. The land of revolution had made me a revolutionary: I would bring a counter-revolution in this land of pseudo-revolution, I vowed mentally.

Thus, I decided to make that land my home. Soon I had a select band of friends, who despite our friendship, had very little in common with me. In retrospect, I wonder what made us stick together? Probably sheer physical proximity. Too much of closeness generates heat – which at times breaks relationships, but at other times also forges them. That must have been the case with me.

These friends of mine, however shallow, tied me down to the land more firmly. As my love for the land increased, an unknown fear also grew within me. I became more humble towards the Big Bird. Soon, my counter-revolution became secondary and my love for my friends became the primary reason for my staying there. It seemed that there was no hope for me to get out of this land. I liked the birds, wanted to be with them, and in turn suffered with them.

Probably, my lessons with M Fay were not yet complete. One day I dreamt of him, requesting me to come back. He asked me what mistake he had made to drive me so far away from him, and so near to these birds. In the morning I decided to be firm with my feathered friends.

'Don't you realise what you are losing by not flying?' I said to an intelligent-looking bird.

'No,' she replied.

'Don't you want to get out of this hole and experience the wide world; the joys of freedom, the pleasure of beating your wings, the power to see things from above?'

'We don't know much about such things. But, what we do know is that if anyone ever tries to fly, or crosses the boundaries, they would be banished forever,' she replied.

'So, what? That would do you real good, you lemons!' My helplessness made me angry and sad at the same time. I also felt guilty about M Fay.

'It can't be,' said the bird. 'This is the land of our forefathers. I love my parents and my friends. I won't survive if I am not allowed to come back. These birds are everything for me. In them lies my freedom and my existence. I wish I was never born with wings. Don't even talk of flying, it's sacrilege.'

It seemed that I had no choice left – these folks were mine now, and I was theirs. I remembered how one year the visiting nightingale at our banyan had arrived with a turkey chick. When we asked him to explain the oddity, he said that during one of his singing tours, he had found this fledgling separated from its mother. Unlike Mr Cuckoo, the nightingale was a compassionate bird (and also a better singer) so he had saved the chick, who now stuck to him like an extra tail. He would have been happy to see the last of Master Turkey, but he was too kind to tell him that. The comic duo became a star attraction. That was my fate now – a comic patchwork of my new friends and me.

My fear seemed to increase in proportion to the number of friends that I made. Now I had to make the Big Bird happy with extra obedience, although he still remained suspicious of me. Whenever I was not watched, I treated myself to the pleasure of flying – mostly at night. My well-wishers would dissuade me, imploring me in whispers not to do so. They loved me and did not want to see me banished.

To cut a long story short, I tried to forget flying and hopped on my legs, as did everyone else. I felt that I was a nobody – not even Tiya the common parrot. I had come out in search of 'myness', and here I was trapped in 'nothingness' – that is what fear had done to me. M Fay continued to haunt me in my dreams

And then, one day I was caught flying by the Big Bird. It was late evening and an intoxicating breeze had made me want to take a spin or two.

'Tiya, come here. What were you doing?' I heard.

'Sorry. I was helplessly tempted by the winds to test my wings. I am truly sorry, sir. '

'Do you know to whom you are speaking, you squirt!' There was a rage in his voice and I quaked in fear. My legs trembled and my mind went blank.

'Yessirthebigbirdsir.'

'Get out of my sight now!'

With fear in my heart, and tears in my eyes, I prayed to be forgiven. But I wasn't. I grovelled on the ground, asking for mercy, but I was kicked out instead. Even my friends stayed indifferent towards me, to save their own feathers. They hardly seemed to know me.

The certainty of losing everything made me fearless now. My dreams were shattered, my hopes were gone and my friends were lost. What could now keep me glued to this stupid land? I mentally thanked the Zarys for what they had taught me unconsciously.

'You foul-mouthed terror machine! Slave driver! Exploiter in the name of dignity and culture – a disgrace on birds! May your wings get arthritic! May you stumble into a pit of coal dust! May lice overrun your body! May you suffer from non-stop itching and sneezing! May your . . .' I screamed out loud.

My friends did not seem to hear or recognise me. With bent heads and quick gait they tried to

look busier than ever. Before flying away I forgot
to spit at the Big Bird.

The Leaktons

'So, Tiya?' I mused to myself. 'With your face
forward and mind backwards, you looked like a
car reversing with its headlights full on.'

I flew in silence with my sad thoughts like
extra baggage. My friends, for whom I had been
struggling and debasing myself, had disowned me
at this crucial hour. The Big Bird, for whom I had
humiliated myself, had kicked me out. And Hans,
on whom I depended, was nowhere near me when
I needed him the most.

Missing your friends? The counter-revolution?
The reform? And if the Big Bird forgave you and
called you back?

Hmm.

Forget it, birdie, life would have been too
monotonous there. Behaving like a flock of
waddling penguins.

Hmm.

Everything is a package deal, my dear. Our
only regret is that we did not spit at the Big Bird.

By refraining, we showed our superior upbringing, right? May he get pharyngitis with all his loud scolding!

We get what we do not want, and we lose what we want. We are here to realise that we are more than what meets our eyes, so let's move forward.

I was charmed at my own gems of wisdom. They were absolutely original. The pinpricks of pain had unlocked my grey cells. I felt better. With a lighter heart, in which sadness still lingered, I reached a new land. The place was even more unkempt than the hair of a teenager. My disorganised mind, however, fitted in well with this new place. It was a welcome change after the organised land of revolutionaries, who were not, however, good at organising themselves. Revolution – my fallen feathers. The cheats!

The inhabitants of this new place seemed to be in some kind of mourning. All I could see around me was people with tears streaming down their sad faces. Their shoulders were stooped, their legs seemed weary, and deep sighs and broken words rent the air. They rested twice as long as they walked, through a fog of pathos that hung thick in the air. Even the trees looked reluctant to grow – their branches hung downwards, their leaves seemed ready to fall and the fruits looked unripe. Compared to the sorrow of the place, my own pain seemed trivial.

A group of locals was moving in a procession. I carefully approached the last of them, and with deep sadness in my voice, I asked him, 'Is someone dead, sir? '

'No.'

'Some serious loss?'

'No.'

'Collective joint pains?'

'No.'

I wondered. What could be the reason behind the sorrow of these creatures, that they leaked tears in gallons? I had always believed that tears were a form of melted foolishness. The more solid stock one had, the more liquid cash of tears could be produced – in gallons and tonnes. Leaktons – that is how I branded them.

I thought the Leaktons may not have enough energy to speak, so I joined the procession to see where it went. I did not have to wait for long. A meeting was on, with a fair number of participants. As one may have guessed, the dais was as shabby as the environment. It reminded me of Mrs Crow's nest, in which one could find the most unnecessary things kept pell-mell. We used to wonder how she could ever locate an object. We also used to wonder if the crow couple lacked the necessities of life, for they were good at pinching things and hiding them perfectly; so perfectly in fact, that they failed to find what they had hidden.

The chairperson was speaking in a tone as limp as a dead rat's tail. 'Citizens of this holy land: We are the chosen people of God to show the denizens of this beautiful world that "Empathy is the key to survival". Every living being is self-centred and thinks only of his or her pain. But we are different. We feel sorry for everything around us and shed tears for them. This is our way of serving the Lord. As has been our practice for years, we will be giving away the "Annual Award for Excellence in Tears" to the citizen who can show us the best way to cry for others. In addition, the winner will be the chairperson for the next year's meeting. Let us begin.' With this, he collapsed in his chair – he was too moved to say another word. There was blowing of noses, sighs, sniffs, and sobs from the audience.

Slowly some of them got off their feet and started presenting their views.

'Existence is so sorrowful, you know. A week ago, I saw a fruit fall from a tree. It made me feel so sad for the tree, as well as the birds on that tree, who would be missing the fruit so sorely. I haven't been able to eat or sleep since then. If you look at any tree around you, you will find umpteen reasons to cry.' The speaker burst into tears and the audience joined him with vehement sniffs.

From a distance I watched each Leakton arise, climb slowly up the steps to the podium, narrate his or her views and receive loud sniffs and sobs from the audience (clapping must have been taboo here). They seemed to have no interest in the award and their speeches continued.

'. . . The previous speaker has greatly enlightened us. I understand how sad it must be for a leaf to fall from a tree – the separation. But think how sad it must be for insects to get caught by the birds – the destruction! How sad it must be for a snake to lose its skin every year – the loss!'

Sobs all around.

'My heart bleeds at the thought of the sorrowful things all around. Have you seen the sun at daytime? We have shelters, but he has no one to save him from the heat. Isn't it so sad? Have you seen the stars at night? Who cares if they might without any reason. Thank you.'

he sound now produced by the audience was
ely confusing. The little that I could make
between their sobs and moans was that they
d to make me a permanent citizen of the
nd also their permanent leader. I was more
illing to do so. What was left in my life now,
han shedding tears and sharing pain?

*ya. There are better things to do in life than to shed tears
d reasons. Get out of this place. Fast.'* It was Hans.
senses had gone numb – I was unable to
act, and Han's words sounded distant. The
of sadness on my wings was too heavy for
-soaked feathers. It was impossible for me
Hans.

urgently repeated himself again. But I felt
s, and hopeless.

hird rebuke and I made a desperate attempt at
t was like waking up dazed from a sorrowful
– my system struggled to shake itself free
ess. With one great effort I was airborne.
ch later, this art of repeated attempts at
vas to save my life. I am grateful to those
umps for the lessons I learnt there. They
me crying, but they also taught me the art
gle. Now I see life as a mixture of sand and

be feeling chilly? Have you felt the wind brushing against your body? Do you realise how tiring it must be for it to keep blowing day and night. Does anybody feel for the wind?'

There were audible sobs. Something had happened to me that made me appreciate the Leaktons' view on life and its problems The pain that I had been carrying from the loss of my friends was now ripe and it leaked out in the form of torrential tears. An important looking Leakton with greying hair and beard all wet with tears, began, 'We are so foolish. Do you realise that the world may end in a black hole soon? Do you feel for all these living things and their offspring? Do you realise that they will not be able to survive? He broke into inconsolable sobs.

The speeches grew more and more outlandish. It was clear that the chairperson was too confused to decide the winner. A really sad Leakton (I could not make out whether it was a he or she) got up, and started, 'I feel blessed to belong to a land and a race that can humbly claim to be the leader in shedding tears . . . (sobs) . . . Having grown up in the rich tradition of many generations of tear-shedding champions, today I have reached a stage where I can shed tears for hours over any

single reason that comes to m
sobs) . . . I can cry because I a
also cry because I did not eat
if I am not honoured with th
shed copious tears if I am awa
Friends, I feel this is empath
the state of perfection in shed
over any given reason. Why
one? (tears).'

Cumulative sighs and sob
chairperson seemed relieve
beat this leaky creature. But,
contended with the unbeatal
been suffering like no one else
pain and frustration drove me t
and I began: 'Citizens of this n
the parrot, and also a charmed
My eyes and tear ducts have I
you. Congratulations for bei
sobbed, making others sob lou
a contender for this excellence
add that I have learnt to live fr
reached a stage where I don't
shed tears. Unlike the previou
want to hurt their feelings by
had named them Leaktons), I

sugar, from which one has to sift out the useful element and exit. I feel that there is nothing in this world for which one may shed tears. Momentary sadness, yes – copious tears, no.

I feel sad for the Leaktons.

Mr Ambiger

*'I am the highest, I am the best
On the top of the 'illi 'iest . . .'*

The satisfied purring of this contented heart sounded like escaping air from a windbag. This was my welcome at the top of the hill, where I had reached after getting away from the leaky-eyed ones. The change was relaxing. There was indeed more to life than making friendships – or shedding tears – I thought. I must achieve something; I must BE something, as Mr Hans had hinted.

The gentleman (I was getting to be more polite) whom I had heard crooning just now, looked like a character straight out of a mythological tale. His garish clothes would have looked outlandish even on an harlequin. His short legs were very powerful, but his stomach appeared extra large. He was something like an oversized pig on the sturdy legs of an undersized horse. He was trying to put on airs, but air seemed to be leaking out of him. I didn't wish to laugh, but my self-control failed me.

'Hey greeno! Where from? Why laugh? Who you?'

His words were funnier than his looks. The few strands of sorrow that were still sticking to my mind, like obstinate bits of chewing gum, came loose. I felt normal again under the healing effect of humour.

Despite his foolish exterior, he had an intelligent interior that was evident from his eyes. I told him the story of my travels, which he heard with great interest. This surprised me, because clever people rarely have the patience for ancient history. Again, to quote Mr Dove, 'The ignorant ones are genuinely interested in what they hear, the sophisticated ones cleverly show interest, and the rest stay indifferent to the tales of others.'

Then the speaker introduced himself. His story was simpler than I had expected. He belonged to the race of Ambigers, whose only aim in life was to reach where my host had reached and was now well settled. Unlike other members of his race, Mr Ambiger had extra powerful legs that he had used for climbing heights, and kicking down the competition. He hated any kind of nearness, and his only relaxation was to sing to himself:

'I am the highest, I am the best
On the top of the 'illi 'iest . . .'

I was not used to this kind of individualistic thinking. Once during my banyan days, Mr Magpie had brought in some trinket filched from a careless bather. The younger amongst us had protested that stolen goods should not be stored in the sacred precincts of the banyan. So to silence us, Mr Magpie had given it away in charity to the young birds' club, on the condition that it would be presented to an outstanding bird every year after an honest competition. It was amazing to see how the birds, who had been shouting against stolen goods, agreed to accept the trinket as the trophy. Weird are the ways of the world, I thought, but engaged myself in organising the competition. Unfortunately, every bird had his or her own speciality; no one was more special than others, and no one was hopelessly bad. So, there was no way of selecting the winner through a fair challenge. Brains were racked and feathers were scratched, but no solution came up. Finally some intelligent bloke suggested that whoever saw the farthest would be the winner. Everyone agreed to this. The competition was held on a pre-announced date. And then horror of horrors – it was found that excepting Mr Owl, everyone could see up to the sun, which was the farthest possible limit. It was then decided that all of us would keep the trinket by rotation for a day and this satisfied us all. Later on, considering Mr Owl's age and good services, even he was put on the register of the trinket's routine round. Even at the time of telling this story, the practice of handing over the prize to the next nest continues.

Coming from such a background, I found Mr Ambiger's attitude quite outrageous and I drew him into a dialogue:

'How do you feel being here, Mr Ambiger?'

'I am the highest, I am the best

On the top of the 'illi 'iest . . .'

This was annoying. One can tolerate someone beating another's drum, but when one beats one's own drum in senseless language, it grates the ears. But probably there was no one to beat Mr Ambiger's drum, so he had to do it himself. I was to realise soon that no one would have praised his achievements, since he had reached the coveted position through sleight of hand and black deeds.

If it were possible, others would have hounded him out of the land.

'I mean, don't you feel lonely here?' I tried again.

'I have chosen to be what I am. External and internal crowding are the same, and equally dangerous. To be alone is a small price to pay if you get what you want to get.'

'Don't you ever want any company?' It was with great tenderness that I remembered my friends at the banyan. They too must be missing me, I thought, and my heart skipped a beat.

'I am not always alone, as you are assuming. Crumb-seeking individuals reach up to me and I give them something. You came to me seeking nothing, so you are different from the others. As a special favour, I am willing to teach you the mantra of reaching the top.'

We birds can reach heights without any tricks. However, I did not want to put him off, and remained silent. He continued, 'Never practise what you preach unto others. This is the mantra to success. Learn this, practise this, dream of this, actualise this in your life, and you will reach my position permanently. Others will look at you with envy, but you will have a sense of fulfilment.'

My outraged reaction was to think of Mr Ambiger's irresponsible ways. What was all this rubbish that he was passing off in the name of cultivating the mind? It was sheer poisonous garbage packaged in the pompous name of 'education'. If I had the choice I would prefer to live and die as a banyan-idiot. One such learned individual could harm the world much more than a thousand uneducated ones. I strongly felt that a universal legislation should be passed to put such fellows on a marooned island. Teachers of humanity – holy sneezes!

I controlled my rage (remembering the Zarys), and tried to enlighten this misguided mind. 'Go back to your roots, sir. Go back. Live as others live. Share your action and words, tears and smiles, with those who are your own. Don't be a blot on your family, friends and community.'

'Blot on what – family, friends and society? I took you for an intelligent bird, but you are as worthless as the other spongies. Know that even in the darkest days of their existence, my friends and family bask in the glory of my name. They themselves cannot achieve glory, but can put on the cloak of reflected glory from me. And, as for society, go down below and see for yourself. You won't be sermonising much after what you see. Go, and I will wait for you.'

I left him, to go and see what was happening below. The mountain had long trails of climbing Ambigers, and everybody appeared eager to reach the top. In a way, their effort was awe-inspiring. Carrying a load and climbing up a narrow and steep trail was not easy.

One climber had nearly reached the top when suddenly another one from below jumped at him. Both fell headlong, far below. I was surprised and hurried to hear what they were saying.

'Why did you do this to me X?'

'Because Mr Y, you think you are great.'

'No, you are a jealous fellow, always doing this to me and to others.'

'Look Y the great! I don't want to repeat the tales of your evil doings. It is a wonder that your body is not aflame with the fire of jealousy that burns in your heart.'

'Enough X, I don't want to blame you. Jealousy and spite is genetic in your family. I must not condemn you for what you have inherited and not earned.'

I could hear sounds of more falls – more allegations and counter-allegations of the same kind. It was too much for my parrot sensitivity. If these climbers wanted to rot in this hole by pulling each other down, let them do so. The very air around was sick. They were all ruining themselves by ruining others. The joy of their own success paled before their pleasure at the fall of others.

I came back to Mr Ambiger who welcomed me with sarcastic words. 'So, greeno! Any more sermons for me? Being a feather bag, you do not realise what a great service I am doing to society by holding on to my high position. If I were to fall below, the floodgates of hell would be opened, and everyone would join the mad struggle to be here. Thank me for everything.'

Mr Hans had said that I, and in fact, anyone, could achieve much more than they thought was possible. Here was a chance for me to be on the highest peak. Should I take it? Was I ready to pay the price for success? Mr Hans? Mr Ambiger? Mr Hans?

I was too confused to decide, so I hurried away from that mad, mad mountain. I thought it prudent to leave such a decision till new developments surfaced. After the Zarys and the Leaktons, I did not want to take the risk of climbing up and then falling headlong. 'Save your feathers Tiya' was my new slogan.

The self-gloating nonsensical words of Mr Ambiger chased me for quite a while:

'I am the highest, I am the best
On the top of the 'illi 'iest. . .'

The Lotos

Lost in my thoughts I was flapping ahead without knowing where I would reach, or what I would experience next. My wishes now centred only at getting some peace and quiet, which my karma had hardly bothered to grant me.

Peace and quiet! I must be getting old, I mused. Movement, be it of the body or mind, is a sign of vitality. When one wants to give that up, one must be very sad, or very tired.

The new land I reached suited my existing mood well. It was peaceful and filled with flowers in bloom and fruit-laden trees. The place appeared free from the crazy creatures whom I had been meeting a bit too frequently. I alighted on an attractive-looking tree. The serenity of the place soothed me, and the safety lulled me into a doze.

Soon a sweet buzz hovering overhead jerked me into alertness. By now I had grown suspicious of things even remotely sweet or attractive, and was convinced that anything sweet had an equal amount of bitterness at its core.

A beautiful butterfly was fluttering around me, and respectfully asked me who I was. She also informed me that she had never seen someone so huge in her life (she seemed completely unaware that her lifespan was less than a month). She told me that she was from a race of butterflies known as Lozos, famous for their colourful wings. I noted that Ms Lozo's whisper-like voice was intoxicating, probably due to her daily diet of the choicest nectar.

Normally I do not like butterflies. These neurotics suffer from an identity crisis; now they are eggs, caterpillar, pupa, and soon, butterflies! They simply cannot decide what to be and what not to be; in less than a month they take all these forms and then fade away from life. They did not do anything worthwhile, except for spreading pollen, and that too after sucking nectar from helpless flowers. I disliked these exploiters on principle.

Knowing that butterflies did not have stings, I felt safe and fearlessly strong. I said, 'I am Tiya, a parrot from a distant land. My fate, curiosity and stupidity have made me homeless, and in return have made me undergo many unwanted experiences. I wish to put a stop to this. Peace and quiet is what I want.'

Ms Lozo was impressed with my voice power that carried far, but was not impressed with my appearance. 'Why do your feathers have only one colour, O Great One? You do have a red ring round your neck, but that does not make you as colourful as we are. You look so odd despite your huge size and booming voice. I have never seen the likes of you,' she said.

One spontaneously tends to indulge in pranks when one stands before a 'lesser mortal'. I had the right mix of intelligence and immaturity, which made me a monster wanting to possess the weak – I was in the grip of the ghoul of mischief.

'Dear Ms Lozo! Variety always branches out from unity, and is an unnatural state. Unity is the mother of everything. Life itself springs from a single cell, and colours are born of a single colour. Everything in its youngest days, including a sapling, has only one colour. This means that variety is a corruption, and unity is greatness. I am great because I am of one colour.'

The foolish Lozo was dumbstruck. Despite the colours she was wearing on herself, she was only a flying insect. Interestingly, my own head was reeling at my arguments. Mr Dove used to say that the best arguments are those which convince not only others, but also oneself.

Ms Lozo burst out, 'Thank you, thank you, Your Greatness! Such a simple thing, and we had never understood it. We are so dumb! You are simply great, O Honourable One! Please allow me a minute to call the other Lozos.'

With all the majesty that I could muster, I looked around and nodded gravely for external show. In my mind, I was very happy, because my conviction that beauty and intelligence were eternal enemies was reconfirmed. Soon Ms Lozo returned with a swarm of butterflies who matched her beauty. She began, 'Your Excellency! You are more powerful than all of us put together, and you have just shown how wise you are. This rare combination of power and wisdom makes you unique. We all bow before you.'

I also bowed to their unbeatable stupidity.

She continued with the request to make me their leader, saying that they would be my slaves for life. Judging by their looks, they were really stupid. Let the game go on, I told myself, and to hide my laughter, I only muttered an occasional 'hmm'.

A new phase of my life had begun. I was powerful, carefree, adored, and at peace. Wherever I went, I was escorted by a band of smart Lozos, who also guarded my nest when I slept. I thought of getting a crown for myself, and also of carrying a cigar in my beak – but finally decided not to indulge my fancies too much.

Then one day the inevitable happened. It was something I had been dreading all along. I felt the invisible presence of Hans near me. His words were stern, 'You are much more than what you think you are, and you can achieve a lot more than you are achieving now.'

The spoilsport.

'What is there to achieve in life other than security and peace, sir? I have both and I want nothing more,' I mumbled.

'You silly nutcracker. Did you leave everything behind, suffer so much and come such a long way, only to stagnate here?'

'This is not stagnation, sir. It's the real way to live life – good food, plenty of rest and enjoyment, and above everything, POWER.

Power is enjoyable; absolute power is intoxicating. In fact, I would advise you to come and stay with me for some days and relax. Nothing like this life, sir.'

Could I hear him breathing hard?

'As you wish, you foolish bird! To complete your enjoyment, I am going to M Fay to tell him of your whereabouts. Soon you will have company. Good luck!'

I did not need any further argument or persuasion. Like waking unwillingly from a pleasant dream, I pulled myself togther and hurried away from the land of the Lozos. M Fay. Holy Feathers! Sugar coated razor – not him again.

The flapping of my wings was now as vigorous as my curses directed at Hans.

The Lollys

During the days before my adventure, I had once overheard two young boys complaining to each other about their school years. 'For how long do we have to wear this silly uniform, carry this heavy bag, get scolded, have short hair and . . .'

'According to my calculations, it might be another eight years, provided you do not flunk!'

Eight years! And we are only ten! I wish I could just run away and play cricket all day!'

'Everyone has to go through this, yaar. Our parents went through it, and our kids will also – at least that's what my dad says.'

'Yes, and I will make sure that my own kids go through this torture. Why shouldn't they suffer if I suffer? After all our parents are making us suffer, isn't it?'

'You don't get it. The other day I heard my parents say that they wanted us to be great people and that is why they have sent us to school. I don't understand what all this fuss is about.'

'But once I become great, I won't be able to do many things. I think I am going to put my pet green frog under my parents' bed sheet tonight. Let's see how great they have become by going to school!'

Frog under the sheet! I had screeched in delight and had flown away. I felt like putting a garland of frogs, strung with a thread of earthworms, around the neck of Mr Hans. My great educator! The only problem was that I was not even sure if Hans had a neck.

'Hi!' It was Hans and I felt embarrassed for my thoughts.

'This is life, Tiya – involvement. Involvement is the key to life, existence, joy and suffering. And once you are out, you are out.'

'I want to get back to my good old banyan. Life was familiar there. My friends must be missing me.'

Silence.

'I was much better the way I was. Enough of these adventures – I want to go back.'

'No, Tiya. You cannot stop now even if you wish to. The game has to go on.'

'For how long?' I moaned.

'Till it is finished – everyone has to go through it. Sooner or later – slowly or fast.'

'You also went through it all?' I was trying to be funny, but sheepishly realised that he was gone.

'Come, see my garden
Better than Eden
Better than heaven.'

The voice sounded firm and confident – even inviting. There was another voice floating through the air as well – equally tempting – softer, but a little less confident.

'Well, well, well
It may also be hell.
Come, my little cutie
Feel its beauty.'

Beauty! My ears pricked up and so did my feathers. The very word was a red signal for lurking danger and the red ring round my neck constantly reminded me of that. I thought of flying away, but my hungry belly and tired limbs were asking for a break. I decided to oblige them, reminding myself to be extra careful.

Alighting on a tall tree, I surveyed the landscape. The place was neat and nice, which was another warning signal for me. What appeared presentable and orderly was far more dangerous than the unkempt and disorganised. Many ills can be safely hidden beneath polish and varnish. The Fays and the revolutionary birds had taught me well.

The land below looked like a patchwork of orchards. There were tall trees without fruits (like the one on which I had perched), and shorter ones laden with inviting fare. What surprised me was the absence of birds, despite the luscious juicy fruits.

The custodians of these orchards were good looking, but had large tongues lolling out of their mouths. These tongues, when in action, were capable of making a clean sweep of anything that came within their reach. I mentally named these creatures Lollys and reminded myself to beware of them. I also decided to watch their activities at first.

Two Lollys were quarrelling over something. I had learnt not to be too curious, so I did not go near them. That was a mistake – soon I was to realise that curiosity also has its value in life. I was feeling hungry and the tree on which I was resting had nothing to nibble. So, I silently descended on to one of the trees in the orchard below. Soon I pierced one of the juicy fruits with my beak – unaware of the lurking danger.

One of the quarrelling Lollys spied me, and his eyes lit up with expectation and greed. It made me pause and think, but I didn't know how to react. The quarrelsome duo began approaching the tree on which I was enjoying my much needed meal. I told myself that I was safe and could fly away the moment I sensed danger.

Suddenly a rabbit ran across the grass.

The Lollys looked at it. There was such menace in their eyes that the terrified little creature became rooted to the spot. A howl of pleasure escaped the throat of one of the Lollys, while a growl of anger emanated from the other.

'Don't try and touch it – that's for me! It belongs to my area.'

'As if you own the entire land!'

'You greedy lolling tongue! Only yesterday we agreed to keep ourselves confined to our own orchards. Why are you eyeing what is rightfully mine? Follow the rules.'

'The weak make laws, while the strong interpret them.'

'What is your interpretation then, fatso?'

'The rabbit intended to run away from your orchard into mine. You can see that he has more sense than you have. Even he knows that I am preferable over you. If he could talk, he would have agreed to be mine. Since he cannot, I must interpret his desires. And be careful not to call me a fatso again. You know the consequences.'

'You fatso, I have heard your arguments too many times in the past. They are staler than your stinking skin. Your store is already full of food, which you can't finish in years. It is rotting away like your rotten values. Why do you snatch what isn't yours? Let me tell you, I will even die fighting to protect my rights.'

'I will wait to see you die. If you want, I can even help you in that. After all, one does not get a chance to serve society everyday.'

'Do you have no sense of justice?'

'What is justice? It is the natural order of things to bring everybody up in society. I am on the top, and it is my duty to bring others to the top. For this I must stay at the top. To perform my duties properly, I must get what I want, and must preserve what I have. Otherwise I will not able to do my duties, which will be a sin. You do not understand these things – that is why you are so wretched.'

My head reeled at these arguments. Mr Ambiger, where are you? Come, learn a few lessons from these Lollys, I messaged him mentally.

The weaker one continued, 'Aren't you afraid of the Almighty who is watching over your dark deeds?'

'I am not doing anything dark. And, now that you mention it, I will sacrifice the rabbit's leg to Him and then eat it later as a sacred offering.'

There was a sudden charge. The weaker Lolly had attacked the stronger one with tremendous force. Their tongues lashed out and got twisted in a knot. It was a strange tongue-tugging war, with howls of anger emerging from their throats.

In the melee, the rabbit awoke from his trance and ran for his life.

I couldn't contain my laughter. 'Bravo rabbit! You were trapped by their external deeds, but freed by their internal thoughts. Lucky you! Run for your life.'

The fight stopped. The eyes that had looked full of hunger earlier were now red with anger. But, I was not afraid. Even if they trapped me, I knew I could fly to freedom. I was sure that greed did not have the power to hold an object. I shouted, 'Hello, sirs! It is good that you lash your tongues at each other. Life would have been difficult for your victims if you reserved your tongues only for them.'

'Wait, I am coming for you,' the dominant Lolly's harsh words rang out.

'Ha, ha! Catch me if you can!' I sang out. Probably he had never seen a bird, and definitely not an intelligent one.

But I had concluded things too early. With determined steps and sweeping tongue, Mr Lolly advanced in my direction. I was alert and got ready to fly higher, beyond his reach.

Higher? It is not easy to fly higher when you are trapped. Without my knowing, I was stuck to the spot from where I had been enjoying the action. I had not realised that the tree had a kind of glue all over it, which made animals, birds and insects stick to it on contact. No wonder, there was not a living thing to be seen around, excepting the Lollys.

'SCREECH . . .' That was the only sound that came out of my throat in this moment of danger. All my intelligence had vanished. My words, wit and humour were now coming out as sweat and fear.

Hans! Where had you landed me? An innocent life was about to be swallowed up by a cruel and greedy tongue – that too for nothing.

I remembered my banyan, my friends, pranks, mistakes, gains and losses. This was the end, Tiya! But was it my fault? I had just been hungry. The Creator had made fruits to satisfy our hunger – so was I wrong in trying to eat one?

My senses were going blank when I felt the touch of the killer tongue. It was like the body of a snake – dry, cold and deadly. It wrapped itself around my body and plucked me from the tree. That was the end – I lost consciousness.

The sudden thud with which I fell brought me back to my senses. Initially I thought that the

Lolly did not like my taste, but soon I realised that there was more to it. The other Lolly had come up from behind and given my captor a fierce kick, thus freeing me with his surprise attack. I flew away, panting and terrified.

My Lolly saviour shouted up at me, 'I had told you that fatso's garden is hell. Come cutie, feel the beauty of my garden. Be my honoured guest.'

Yes, experience safety in the belly of this demon! How could he imagine that I would come down a second time? Despite my physical and emotional upheaval, I flew away. I just wanted to be safe. I don't know why, I felt the silent presence of Mr Hans around me. I was too drained to talk, and probably he wanted me to recover through my silence.

The Dingdings

My mind resembled a violent, angry ocean with thoughts as turbulent waves – each a product of the previous one, which in turn gave birth to new thoughts. Some of these were insignificant, while others were overwhelming. There seemed no way of curbing this angry ocean as each wave was adding to its agitation. I wondered why I had to experience the danger of death when I had not asked for it? After all, I was just hungry and had eaten for survival. But how could one survive in a place where the very struggle to exist could blow away one's chances of survival? Every feather of my body and every cell of my brain, however small, was sobbing with pain.

From where I was flying (not very high), I could hear the loud noise of cheering and shouting. I didn't pay any attention. My hunger, pain, fear and dejection made me indifferent to things around me.

I remembered how once I had seen some odd looking humans resting under my good old banyan tree. I had rushed to Mr Woodpecker to figure out about them. He had explained that these were holy men who had seen through the vanities of the world and had become indifferent to its charms. I was neither impressed nor convinced, but rather, rubbished the whole idea. In those days I felt that attraction was normal, and indifference was vanity. Whenever we birds quarrelled (and we did this a lot), a temporary indifference overwhelmed us, but it did not last long. How could these holy men stay aloof from the world forever? There had to be more to it than met the eyes, I had felt. But now my perception was changing. The blows that I was receiving were making me indifferent to the charms of the world.

I had been airborne for too long and my wings needed rest. But after my experience with the Lollys, I was wary of every tree. Imagine my predicament! My natural resting place was a tree, and now I was scared of every one of them that stood on the ground. How was I going to live the rest of my life if I had to be suspicious of every leafy green shelter? I taxied myself to a halt on a branch, and edged my beak towards a berry – softly – carefully. And I waited to watch the effect – my body intact, my brain alert, and my feet free.

I was intending to fly away, when there was a commotion below. An unusual sight greeted me. I landed on a lower branch to bring myself nearer to the new arrivals who looked like human beings, but with very long noses. They were all engaged in combat with each other's noses. It looked something like 'nose wrestling', Their noses were muscular, powerful and longer than their arms, and these folks were using them for both pushing and puffing.

Slowly others came to watch the wrestling and to cheer. All of them had noses of varying lengths, ranging from the slightly long to simply awesome specimens. The cheering brought fresh vigour in the wrestlers.

'Bravo Y, beat that fellow! You are younger and have nothing to lose, not even your honour.'

'Remember X, defeat of the longer is worse than death.'

'Come up Y. Glory in victory, dignity in defeat. Down with X!'

'Cheer up X. Push hard to retain your crown. Down with the upstart!'

The atmosphere had heated up. Noses twitched all around. I felt it was futile to talk to the boisterous crowd, so I approached a decent looking denizen whose nose was on the shorter side. I cautiously asked him what was happening. He explained, 'X considers himself to be the king of noses, a fact that has got him some admirers and followers. Y, on the other hand, is younger and has a fairly long nose that is still growing. This has made X declare that Y must keep his nose covered with a cloth – jealousy, you know. Y thinks otherwise and so he has collected a band of lackeys who have raised the slogan "Death to the old nose, life to new dreams". As you can understand, it is the eternal rivalry between the old and the new. Right now the matter is being decided in the open, and not for the first time.' My new friend also explained to me that they were a race called Dingding – affluent, peace loving, but slightly sensitive about their noses.

'That's so silly,' I couldn't help saying.

'It is a matter of honour,' said Mr Dingding sagely.

'Silly,' I persisted.

'Honour is life, to surrender means death.'

'Silly,' I continued at a loss for words.

'You are ignorant about the ways of the world.'

'Silly,' I insisted.

'Where are you from? A creature with no culture . . .' Before he could continue further, there was a commotion. X and Y had both lost their balance and fallen on their backs. They now looked so funny that I could not contain my tittering. But even before I could complete my full quota of laughter, I saw Mr Y Dingding get up and pounce on Mr X Dingding. Mr Y's nose hit the ground before his body could hit Mr X. He howled with pain, lost his balance, and fell backwards. The story was repeated with the other one on top now and the same comedy routine was acted out.

The battle had now spread from Y to A who had been accidentally hit; and then A hit B and so on . . . it was like a wildfire on dry grass. Soon very few spectators were left, which resulted in less cheering. The fighting simmered down and it was now time for disentanglement and the parting shots.

'If only I were not in a hurry! I would have sawed off your nose.'

'That is what you always offer as an excuse. Remember how I have always battered your nose to pulp.'

' It's just a matter of time till I level it with your face. The whole world knows of your family as the beaten nose ones.'

I wondered what they were fighting for? What did they gain by displaying such worthless vanity? Were they trying to hide some kind of weakness behind the mask of honour? I asked my guide, 'Don't you have difficulty walking with your long noses? Don't you get stuck in smaller spaces?'

'Yes. But, there is one's honour to be considered. People kill their own kin to save the honour of their family. Even a snake raises its hood when one tramples upon its tail.'

'Indeed Mr Dingding,' I said. 'The tail is the right place for one's honour to reside in. It should not move ahead of one.' I was pleased with my words, for he was silenced.

'I feel so sad at your plight, sir,' I continued in a smug tone.

'It is a matter of honour,' Mr Dingding repeated. 'What would one's life be without honour? Useless.'

'Honour doesn't allow you to lead a normal life of peace and contentment, and yet you talk of honour! Nitwits.'

'You yourself are a nitwit, sir. Where are you from, you undignified soul?'

'I am a parrot. That too not an ordinary . . .'

I had to stop mid-sentence. My beak tickled and I felt it growing a little longer. I immediately came back to my senses and thought it better to keep quiet. After all, I was a bird. Of what use was honour or a long beak to me? I would be sitting on the ground, and my beak would be touching it! Better leave this place quickly instead of poking my short 'nose' in the problems of the long-nosed ones. The Dingdings could make all the din with the hollow ring of their honour, I was happy the way I was.

I left the place in a hurry. Even today, my beak is a little longer than it used to be – a reminder of my one-time vanity.

The Skato

I felt completely numb after I flew away from the land of the Dingdings. My emotions were flat – like the landscape below that looked as appealing as a hostile host on a cold winter evening. When frustration combines with aversion, the result is complete detachment. This led to my absolute indifference to what lay below me. Once in a while, I even 'hmm'd' to no one in particular to express my annoyance at everything in this world.

I realised that whatever was happening around me, was due to a chain of events. Things in this world came gift-wrapped in circumstances, which when opened, created newer circumstances – mostly unfavourable. If one wanted to be successful, one had to mould the circumstances according to one's needs. I had to do something about it.

I now felt the urge to be a teacher. As a fledgling, I had heard a bit about teaching and training. But it wasn't clear to me about who taught whom. To know more about this, I had once approached Mr Dove and his explanation was quite simple: 'Teaching is mostly about cheating. It is a way in which fools make fools of other fools, in an intelligent way. This makes teaching the easiest job in the world.' I was aghast by his words. 'Mr Dove, are you sure about what you are saying?' I asked. 'I am an ignorant parrot. Does that mean that I too can become a teacher?'

It would be quite some time before I realised that he was correct in his own way, at least about

himself. Why else would he go on behaving like
a capable teacher? But I was green in those days,
and even quite ambitious. My heart was filled with
hope at his words, and I had asked him, 'What is
the best way to teach, Mr Dove?'

'Always tell others to do what you actually
don't do yourself. This is the secret of teaching,'
and with these words he had flown away. Excited,
I had sped to Mr Woodpecker to tell him what I
had learnt. On hearing what I had to tell him, Mr
Woodpecker strongly advised me to be careful of
the company I kept. He added that wrong ideas
in immature minds were a recipe for disaster. I
had respected his advice till date, but something
was blocking the clarity of my perceptions just
now. My eagerness to be a teacher, had driven
away every ounce of sensibility that is expected
of someone in this profession.

Soon I was to make a fool of myself.

A green jungle arose in the path of my flight. I
didn't have to be cautioned that something strange
was about to take place. Going by the trend of
events, something had to happen quite soon. This
time, I was determined to preach to the ignorant
about the higher things in life, come what may. I
even decided to be firm with the stubborn ones.

If not a hard peck with my beak, I would at least direct a disapproving glance at the unworthy ones.

I glided to a halt on a leafy branch that was well-hidden. Below every tree sat elegant- looking creatures with a fixed upward gaze. Their necks were elongated and stiff, something like a baby giraffe's, secured by a collar. Even when these creatures moved, they stared with their faces upwards. We birds prefer looking ahead or below, and rarely look up. Why were these fellows looking up, when there was so much to see down below? I anticipated something would happen soon to explain it all, and braved myself for it.

I remembered the day when a group of people once took shelter under our banyan tree. They were quite strange in their behaviour. One of them used to walk on a rope, while another did somersaults. Then one day I found that one of their lads who used to walk on his hands, was actually carrying a plate of food on his legs. I racked my brain, but could find no explanation. Finally I approached Mr Woodpecker, who explained that they were acrobats who lived by performing difficult antics. But to be honest, I am still not clear why anyone would want to interchange the role of his limbs. The situation here was something like that.

The trees around us were fruit-laden and attractive. Many fruits lay spread on the ground under the trees, but no one was paying them any attention. The fellows sitting under the trees had their sights set too high, and their melancholic eyes were filled with desire and hunger.

As was my habit, I engaged the host below my tree in a friendly chat.

'How do you do?'

'How do you do?'

'Nice place, isn't it?'

'Yes, but cruel.'

I failed to see any cruelty, but kept silent. He then asked me about myself, my life and my achievements, and I told him all that was worth telling in brief – hinting that I had nothing to boast of. This cheered him up, and in turn, he told me that they were a race called Skazo, superior to every other race in the universe because they always looked up. 'Down is degrading, up is uplifting' was their social motto, a violation of which could invite severe punishment.

'Gutter-brains,' I muttered beneath my breath, making sure that he could not hear. 'How is life in general?' I tried once again.

'Not really good.'

'The place seems attractive enough to me.'

'I am not able to get what I want, and have to go hungry for days.'

This surprised me. With all the ripe fruits around, it was impossible for anyone to starve, unless one chose to do so. I enquired about his health, which he said was perfect. Could I be of any help to him, I asked? He hesitated, but finally spoke out: 'Could you please help me get the fruit that I wish to have? I can point it out, provided you agree not to take that for yourself. Folks cannot be relied upon, you know.'

'You have many fruits all around you. What is so special about that fruit, Mr Skazo?' I tried to be a patient teacher.

'As I told you, I have set my eyes on it since it was a small bud. I want to have it. That is that.'

What a fool to leave what is, and desire what is not. The teacher inside me was coming out in full blaze.

'Mr Skazo, eating is important, not the fruit. Never want what is not; be happy with what you have. Just look at yourself. How much time, energy and emotion you are wasting on a silly thing like that. You could have used all of that to make yourself a better Skazo. Throw away your ignorance and grow up. It is never late to begin – start now.'

'That is your view, parrot-brain. Why must we, the cleverest among animals, listen to a word-repeater?'

I was rattled. Here I was, basking in the glory of my newly-found role, and he was treating me like anybody else. What would happen to the good old world if everyone started behaving like this? I was offering my services for free and he was not even appreciating it! If I had not visited the land of statues and known the dangers of anger, I would have burned him down with a single glance. But I only said, 'Be practical. What you have is good enough. What is unreachable may not be good. It might even be worm-eaten.'

'So what? I will have what I want. The strong willed do not change their decisions everyday.'

It was meaningless to soft pedal, so I decided to assert myself. 'Fine. It's your headache, provided you have a head. Take what you want. Climb and get it. Why trouble me?' I said.

'You can see that we cannot climb trees, and you are still making fun of my helplessness. It is unfair to laugh at anyone's misery. Help, if you can; stay away, if you can't. Just don't sermonise.'

There were tears in his sad eyes. I felt sorry, but remembered his irreverence, and also that I needed to make him a better being.

'What you need *is* sermons, and that is why I am giving them to you. I can indeed help you, but before that you must understand why it is wrong to behave the way you are behaving.'

'You are the ladder between me and my goal. Instead of giving me what I want, you are giving me sermons.'

As chance would have it, the marked fruit fell from the tree. Mr Skazo gave a cry of joy and stretched out his hands towards it. But he lost sight of the fruit because he would not look down – and having missed it, became sad once again. He calmed down, and set his eyes on a different fruit. The same requests continued to be made about the fruit. I could not contain myself and blurted out, 'You are like a monkey, Mr Skazo; setting your eyes on something new every moment. See how fickle you are! Maybe, one brags about what one lacks. Why else would you keep talking about the ideal? Learn not to look only beyond, but also around you.'

There was something magnetic about this land. Now that I am able to look back at the events impersonally, I feel that the place had the power to imprison every mind and restrict its ability to perceive correctly. My own mind was growing dull and my reasoning was losing its edge. My perspective was altering too – if I saw red, instead of seeing the colour, I saw danger. Similarly when I saw an object, I saw it as something that one should acquire. I had stayed too long on these slippery grounds, and it was time for me to move.

The fruit didn't remain a fruit anymore for me. It was now an object that I needed to have for myself. I reached the branch, from which it was hanging and spoke, 'Since you are not able to get this fruit, it means that you are not destined to get it. There has to be a better candidate for this than you. And, who is a better choice than me? Not only can I look up, but I can also look around. In addition, the situation favours me – so I will have it. Thanks for pointing out this fruit to me. You are good at starving, so continue with that.'

'You brute of a bird! Leave it alone. Don't be cruel to me.'

'Be satisfied with my thanks, you stiff-necked sky gazer. Others won't even offer you that.'

I still wonder what had possessed me. My desire to be a teacher was gone. Instead, I was just another waster. Was it the irrationality of the land? Was it just fun gone out of hand on my part? I proceeded to peck at the fruit, when, BOOOOOM!

It must have sounded much softer to the others – since the sound had come from my own self, it seemed louder to me. My head reeled in its effort to balance my body that had been thrown into a spin by a rotten apple flung by Mr Skazo. Obviously he had lowered his sights for a moment to pick up the fruit – which meant that I had had some success as a teacher. But this small success was no consolation for the pain that was shooting inside me.

I find it difficult to narrate what happened after that. The pain in my left wing, where I had been hit, was enormous. I flew with agonised shrieks – directionless – downwards – and ended in a sharp fall.

Iceberg Riders

So, Mr World Teacher?
Hmmm.
Straw head with the I.Q. of an egg.

Hmmm.

Let us hope that our career as a teacher ends here.

Hmmm.

How could you be so undignified?

Everyone does such things once in a while. Probably the land had something to do with my undignified behaviour.

How could you forget that values practised in favourable conditions are not values? And that morality is born only when values are practised in adversity.

Yes, I know this, and have tried to practise it in the past. So what if I slipped once? Morality should not be judged by the failures, but by successful attempts one has made. The past is past, let us be careful not to stray again.

In brief, that is how my mind was wrestling with itself to get out of its guilt. I had always sheltered under a strong moral cover, thus any chance crack in it unnerved me terribly. What I had done with Mr Skazo was unpardonable in my own eyes.

The pain in my left wing dazed me and made my flight path unsteady. I eagerly wanted to land somewhere, but as luck would have it, there was no tree or safe perching place in sight. I continued to fly, till I could hardly see in the evening darkness.

'No risk, no gain, moron! I also wish to add that it is only the foolish who fall. Our motto is "Calculate correct and stay perfect". The more the foolish ones fall, the better it is for all. The genetic pool of stupidity will diminish – nature will have less to nurture.'

I could hardly guess what sort of future these animals would have, or what their futuristic society would be like. Drunk with overconfidence, these lambs would sink in order to check the correctness of their calculations! I should have flown away at that, but my injured limb failed me. I needed to stay here to recover. And like every other compulsion in life, my compulsion was dragging me to danger.

I continued, 'Do you have any other option apart from riding these contraptions, sir?' I was worried for my safety.

'Why not? We have a whole range of boats attached to these bergs. But, there is no charm in using them. The joy of riding an iceberg is the joy of freedom and power.'

'Don't you ever worry about your own safety?' I ventured to ask.

I needed no answer; there was another 'CRASHHHH'.

Finally I landed on an island, which had only small clumps of vegetation. There was no reason to panic, I told myself, and went off to sleep with pain shooting out from my body and mind. Night and its accompanying buddy, sleep, enveloped me soon.

The next morning I welcomed the new sun with a warm heart. The tight embrace of sleep had made my body and mind fit to welcome the new day. You must be surprised how I had forgotten my past bitterness, and had once again become the lively young parrot of the banyan. In hindsight, I feel that probably we are programmed to live in the present, and that is why we tend to forget the past, or think of what might happen in the future.

I tried to figure out why I suddenly felt unsteady, and looking around me I found that what I had taken to be firm ground, was actually a group of islands floating loosely in a vast expanse of water. Scattered here and there were a few small houses fronted by potted plants and shrubs. Wandering about in this landscape, were the strangest-looking creatures, somewhat like lambs on two legs. I got curious, but decided against investigating further. I knew that something would go wrong if I tried to be too inquisitive. However, I didn't have to wait to be curious – the unnerving sound of a great crash sucked me into the midst of the action automatically.

We birds cannot stand sudden explosions. I looked left and then right, and was horrified to see that one of the islands had split into two. I then realised to my horror that this was not a group of islands, but a collection of I-C-E-B-E-R-G-S! These crazy creatures were riding icebergs to reach wherever they were trying to go! The survivors from the crash were somehow rescued by the others, wet and frozen.

Parrots are not considered to be wise, but we do know quite a few facts. I had heard about icebergs and remembered them quite well. It is a funny thing about memory that whenever one is in a crisis, every bit of information associated with it rushes to the front.

I addressed the nearest lamb, 'Good morning, Mr Lamb.'

'I am not Mr Lamb. Don't attach unworthy names to me. I deserve the best.'

'I am sorry, sir. How may I address you?'

'Cut it out, pompom. Say what you want.'

This creature was more abrasive than a chainsaw.

'Sir, this is an iceberg, isn't it?'

'Yes, it is an iceberg. So?'

'Don't you think it is a bit dangerous to ri

'Dangerous – what danger can there be? F is the noose of the weak, courage is the ornam of the strong.'

I sincerely wished he had met the Big B in the flightless land, then he would have kno what fear was. Even the very memory of him ma me sweat. However, I controlled the drift of n thoughts and focussed on the present.

'I mean, you might get drowned. Icebergs kee melting, don't they?'

'It is a calculated risk. Ever heard of that, y stuffed olive? You are as green inside as you a outside.'

My past experiences had made me strong so I ignored the jibe. In my greener days, I m have reacted strongly.

'You make calculations to enter a risk, Aren't calculations supposed to take the risk awა

He didn't understand the irony, and continu 'One must take a risk if one has to be somethi you cowardly feather-ball.'

'Won't falling in these waters freeze you death?'

Our own iceberg had split into two, creating huge waves all around. Mr Lamb (as I preferred to call him mentally) was in the cold water. He looked quite silly and shouted, 'Save me..eee.'

'Come on, sir!' I squawked, 'Hold on to my leg tightly, and you will be safely out. You are in the safe legs of Tiya. Hold on!'

Enthusiasm born out of overconfidence can be fatal. What followed was tragic – and also comic. Imagine a lamb holding the leg of a parrot and trying to come out of the water! Naturally, what happened after that was a foregone conclusion.

I fell into the freezing waters – wet and cold – sinking to my death.

A frantic rescue operation began. Mr Lamb was pulled out to safety by the other members of his clan. But I remained where I was – down and below – drowning. Obviously no one seemed to know me, or even care. As on previous occasions, I started to philosophise. This is life, I thought. You go an extra mile to save someone, but get the stick in turn.

By a stroke of unnatural luck, I was rescued by two fishermen in a boat. I don't remember much of anything after that, and don't want to recollect what little I remember. I asked the fishermen how I could repay my debt of gratitude, and what I was told came as a thunderbolt.

'You need not be grateful to us, rather it is we who are grateful to you. We have been catching and eating fish for many days. Now we will now cook you in a curry for a change,' they said in glee.

'Don't take it hard, my friend,' one of them continued. Even otherwise you were as good as dead. At least you will now have the consolation of having served someone well. Cheer up – you are going to be remembered by us forever.'

My choked emotions did not allow a single word to emerge from my beak, but my thoughts were as active as ever. I remembered how crocodiles ate their victims and then shed tears. These demons were something like that. Hypocrites!

'This is life, Tiya,' I told myself, 'You are saved only to be sacrificed by the saviour!'

That is when my saviour-killer's partner broke out, 'Are you going to use garlic in that ditch water curry of yours?'

'How did you guess that, brother? It would be an insult to our friend to be cooked without the proper masala.'

'Don't poison the curry with garlic. What you cook is bad enough.'

'I will do what I want. The bird is mine, and I will cook it the way I want.'

Making his intentions clear, he caught hold of my wet feathers, and putting me in the cooking pot, fixed the lid on firmly. I struggled to come out, but my soaked feathers did not help.

'Boil Tiya. You are more than what you thought you were! Did you ever guess that you could be the essential ingredient for a curry? This is the great achievement that the wise Hans hinted at!'

I bade goodbye to life, asked pardon from all those I had hurt in any way, and closed my eyes

– when suddenly there was a resounding crash. Probably the partner had kicked the pot in his rage. I shot out of the vessel, where I had been warmed by the water, and ducked for my life.

The last I saw of them was that they were at each other's throats for having let their prize catch go. I also heard a crash of another island breaking up. Unmindful of all this, I swiftly flew away, never to look back. I was subdued, calm and silent – changed forever.

Part III

With Hans

My mind wasn't in control anymore. It was racing wildly and towing my body in its wake, which was trying to totter after it like a doting mother suffering in the hands of her spoilt and unpredictable child. Looking back on those days, I feel sorry for my body, which had to suffer so much just to be near its dear one, my mind.

As I flew on with my wings flapping wildly, the familiarity and security of my good old banyan seemed like the remote past. Like any one with a bright future, I had no time for history. New experiences had forced me forward onto newer experiences, and in the process, the old ones were getting faded and overwritten.

The rush of events had telescoped my sense of time, and the details in my memory had grown jumbled into each other. At that time, I was only conscious of the fact that it was impossible for me to stop or turn back. So far, whenever I had wanted to stay at a place, I was forced away – and whenever I had wanted to fly away from something, I was forced to stay a little longer. I was like a young student going on an educational tour in a speeding bus, who had the freedom to move inside the bus, but not the freedom to get off – while new sights kept appearing and vanishing unexpectedly and quickly. Although I was learning through my experiences, I felt cramped and longed for freedom, which was nowhere in sight.

Every adventure that I had encountered was unique, I mused, and each experience through which I had passed seemed to take my personality apart, shake it clean, and put it back together to make me a new parrot. Physically I had not changed much, but internally I had changed a lot – and permanently. All this was due to the five simple words of Hans: 'You are no ordinary parrot.' Simplicity must be a living power – the almighty Lord must be a simple bird with even simpler words.

That is how my thoughts got centred around Hans. I wondered if he was wrong about me. In that case, all that I had faced would be a total waste. But, which sane bird would go through such nerve wracking experiences knowingly? I consoled myself with the thought that knowing Hans was worth the trouble. It was better to know someone like him and suffer, than to stay safe and not know him.

'Nice to see that you remember me once in a while.'

It was Hans – think of him and he was there. That is what I had always experienced in the past. He was like a forgotten part of one's body, which suddenly became prominent when one focussed on it. It had been ages since I had heard him. That wasn't his fault, of course. I had not thought of him seriously for quite a while, except when cursing him occasionally. I guess, like anyone else, Hans also preferred not to come forward when an ugly outburst awaited him. But the fact remained that despite my sudden outbursts against him, only he seemed familiar and dependable. In the rush of events, when everything else was like a passing sight, he alone was permanent.

If only he had a form!

My excitement at having him by my side melted away all my pain, which now trickled like two rivulets from my eyes. I was not sure if Hans, with his perpetual state of bodilessness could see me – so I continued to fly. Probably that was the best way for me to regain normalcy after all the lunacy that I had been facing.

I alighted on a tree to make my body and mind stable. Slowly the memories of the lands that I had crossed started losing their sting. I was filled with the kind of peace experienced by a person who had escaped unharmed from a dark pit full of deadly snakes. The peace was coloured by joy – sheer joy.

Hans continued, 'You are wondering why you are different? Actually no ordinary bird would survive these experiences. Any other bird would either stay trapped in one of these lands, or perish. A few would survive one or two of these adventures, but would go around beating their drums loudly about their very ordinary achievements. Indeed you are special – you will realise it soon.'

My smile became wider, but more humble at the same time. People do not realise that the best way to make a person bow his head is to praise him. To break the silence, Hans asked, 'Anyway, how was your journey?'

'You seem to know everything, so why ask?' My reply was soft. My mind was experiencing a calm that I had never known earlier. It was the calm after the storm.

'You sound so tranquil?'

In the past I would have fended off such personal comments with scorching words. No more – I just smiled. Experience gives knowledge, and knowledge is strength. Strength is peace, and I was at peace.

'Tiya, while climbing a peak, you go up and also down. The essential thing is to keep moving – climbing up and down are irrelevant in the journey of life.'

Childishness is a difficult habit to get rid off – I still carried a vestige of it – and so I looked up and then down to irritate Hans. However, unlike previous occasions, I did not ask him a foolish question. I knew that if one delayed one's reactions just for a moment, a lot of calamities could be avoided. In the days when I believed in quick action, I used to agree with Hans only to maintain peace, but now it was different. Instead of making a wisecrack, I said, 'Sir, I wish to get out of all this. I wish to lead a normal life once again. Only you can help me out of this web.'

'Hmmm.'

'I have been obedient to you, and will continue to be so. Grant me this one favour.'

'Tiya, you are on the way to your banyan. If you reach there you will see that you are a different Tiya. So, hold on.'

I was not sure what he meant by a 'different' Tiya. Would my feathers turn red? Would I get the voice of Mr Eagle, whom we all feared so much? It was all quite puzzling. So, to clarify matters, I put the question respectfully, 'Sir, will I start speaking a different language?'

'If by language you mean the parrot language, it is not going to change. You will know the change when it comes.'

'At least help me hasten the process.'

Hans paused – unusual of him. His words had always seemed to race like fiery horses – impossible to be reined. I felt happy and strong to stop them in their tracks.

'Very well, come along. But from now on you must not react to anything that you see, hear, touch, feel, or experience. Let things take their own course. Just watch them arrive, stay and leave. Reaction causes involvement, which in turn makes you smile and cry, which in turn makes you react further, and entangles you more in its affairs. Stay indifferent. Involvement kills, indifference frees.'

I felt astounded. What Hans told me made sense, but it seemed too deep. I ventured, 'Sir could you suggest something a bit more exciting?'

'Yes, of course. You can continue on your usual route. You may even love the millions of beings you have not yet met and who are waiting for you. Happy journey, birdie.'

My heart quivered so violently that it made my body shudder hard, and I hastily said, 'I promise to do as you say, sir.' I wondered how the tree on which I was perched did not collapse. Even if Hans was tricking me, he was a master trickster. But it was better to be with such a master. He did not have to take lessons in the art of persuasion – his one word was enough to make anyone fall in line. I flew on confidently with invisible Hans by my side – to new lands and new adventures.

The Crystal Cage

We – Tiya and Hans – travelling in silence.

Hans had asked me not to interact with anyone anymore. I was only supposed to watch. 'Stay away from everyone, everywhere,' was my motto now. Silence seemed to improve my powers. I felt relaxed, calm, able to understand things better, and in general, capable of laughing things away. There was no harm in practising something that was doing me only good. I remembered the episode of the queen bee at the banyan.

There was an extra large beehive on the banyan where I lived. The queen of the hive was a pompous and silly bee. And why not? After all, there were a million bees under her command who continuously buzzed around her, fawned upon her, gave her the best nectar, looked after her needs and comforts, and felt privileged to do any little thing that they could for her. The care made her body glow with unmatched radiance, and loaded her mind with extreme dullness; what she gained in beauty, she lost in intelligence.

At times I felt jealous of this witless queen bee, but consoled myself with the thought that it was better to be a brainy bird than a parasitical beauty. And, what was the fun in drinking the same nectar day after day? Much later I would realise that aversion to nectar was something that characterised parrots.

It so happened that once there was an outburst of ferocious buzzing among the bees. By nature, they are foolish and seem to buzz around unnecessarily, but that day it seemed as if dynamites had exploded inside their little heads and hive. I genuinely felt sorry for them. Then we came to know from the excited Mr Hummingbird (their arch rival) that the queen, despite her superior diet and supreme privileges, had fallen ill. 'Serves Her Majesty right,' I thought. 'Living off the labour of others! It is natural for baby birds and animals to be fed by their mothers, but kings and queens never seemed to grow up – they demanded to be fed by others all their lives. Self-dependence was something they neither practised, nor knew. '

The helpless bees were in a frenzy. The beating of their wings was driving everyone at the banyan crazy, but finally a diagnosis was made. The prescription was dire: Her Majesty was to come out of her palatial suite, fly down to a medicinal plant, and take a sip of its bitter sap. With great reluctance she took the bitter medicine, so that she could continue enjoying her sweet diet.

I told myself that I could also do what the queen bee had been forced to do. I could also act against my nature to gain strength. If silence helped me, I would practise that. Mr Woodpecker used to say that 'clear reasoning gives clear understanding, which in turn gives a firm resolve.' I had always felt that that was the best way to increase one's will power. The crows and pigeons living in our banyan were a hopeless lot, simply because they had no clear understanding of what they wanted.

'See these folks, Tiya,' Hans whispered.

My body gave a violent start. Invisibility has its own problems – you forget that your companion is around, and when the voice suddenly erupts from nowhere, you tend to get startled.

I looked around to see that the inhabitants of this place were all looking upwards at something, with great longing. I also looked up, and saw a large goblet, studded with precious gems, hanging in mid-air. How could that be? How could an object hang by itself in space?

Before I could get an answer to the riddle, I saw a few of the young fellows take a run up, and make a dash to reach the goblet. But they would fall down with a thud, and lie face down for some time before getting up. There seemed to be deep gashes and cuts on the bodies of these fallen heroes. I observed that they periodically went to a first aid centre, applied balms to their wounds, and got ready for the next jump.

The place was all about jumps and falls, so I asked Hans about it.

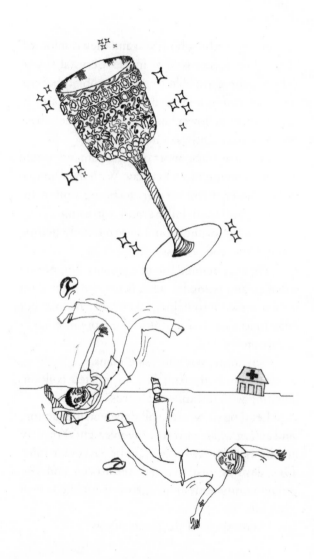

'It is something both you and they cannot see, Tiya. The goblet is kept inside a crystal tower. These people are able to see the goblet, but not the transparent and hard crystal that encases it. The protecting tower has sharp spikes which cause more damage to these innocent folks.'

On an average, most of these jumpers would be experiencing two falls a day. With their limited brain power, there seemed to be no option for them other than falling and suffering. They were aiming for the moon, but were only getting wounded in the process.

'Sir, they remind me of the Skazos, ignoring what is, and going for what is not. I do not want to get drawn into helping these silly people, but may I just say a few words to the more intelligent ones here?'

'Stay away, stay safe,' said Hans.

'Sir, my body feels like an inflated balloon, bursting with unexpressed words.'

'Let it be so. Words will draw you into action, and action will lead you to involvement. You may not be as lucky as you were in the past every time. One dash against the invisible tower, and you would continue dashing against it for the rest of your life.'

I hurried out of the place quietly.

Tails Aflame

I had always felt that adventures lose their charm when you are not a participant. But now that I was with Hans, my perspective was gradually changing. I was realising that watching could be better fun than joining in the game.

The folks of the new land where we reached next, had short tails of fire that burned with varying vigour. I wondered where these tails got their fuel supply! To save themselves from accidental burns, they used metallic jackets that did not seem very effective.

They seemed to be nice folks, but whenever they moved around, there was the possibility of their flaming tails igniting things. And that is what was happening. Every now and then a house was erupting into flames, which gave the place a constantly fiery look.

Whenever a fire broke out, several of these blazing-tailed creatures, including the one responsible for the fire, rushed to put it out. With great shouts of enthusiasm, they focussed their body and soul on the noble act of saving others. Their coordination was so perfect that they would have shamed us individualistic birds.

However, if their intention and effort was praiseworthy, their actions were ridiculously futile. In the process of putting out the fire, they invariably put more houses on fire. Starting a fire, and then putting it out, were the twin occupations of these good natured souls. In between, they nursed their burn injuries.

Naturally it was difficult for me to restrain myself.

'Sir, are these people the solution to the problem, part of the problem, or the problem behind the problems? They remind me so much of the Fays – loving, but dangerous.'

'Tiya, think, and you will realise that you are also like them. Nearly all acts of charity, kindness and service are like this. You first place someone in a problem, and then dive in to save him. And, now we better make a move, before your tail also starts spitting fire.'

Hans was right. Quite often, I irritated Mr Owl and then took extra steps to soothe and calm him down. I felt embarrassed, and tried to look away from where Hans could have been.

I had no desire to see flames coming out of my tail and so I hurried away.

The Donkeys on the Run

'What is there in a donkey's life? What is there in a donkey's life?' We were greeted by this monologue of a trotting donkey at the farm that we had reached. Donkeys are a peculiar breed; they can neither be led by a ring in their nose, nor can they be pulled by a rope round their neck. They can only be driven by a stick from behind, or led forward by their changing moods. Their obstinacy can only be matched with their stupidity.

The donkey that we saw below was in a motivated mood. Soon I was to see that all the donkeys of the land were equally hyperactive – they were running around, trotting or cantering for no particular reason.

I watched them in amusement. When one donkey went to eat a clump of green grass, he could only snatch a mouthful before he began to run again; and when another donkey went for a drink of water, he could spare just enough time for a sip. Action, action, action. I wondered if a horde of bumblebees were after their tails.

'What is there in a donkey's life? We must be more, much more than a donkey,' an animal cried aloud once again. He had noticed my presence, and was now addressing me. Interestingly, even while he was speaking, he was running around the tree where I was perched lazily.

'What a fine fellow you are! Sitting quietly and doing nothing – not even replying, you lazy zombie!' said Mr Donkey to provoke me into speech.

What did he know of my life? How would he know what a great doer, talker and thinker I had been in my time? Had I not won the award for talking for hours on no topic at all, at the banyan? That too when I was a mere chick? It was only later that Ms Cuckoo defeated me in an unfair duel. Wasn't I the leader and member of many movements, councils and forums of the birds at our banyan? I had achieved and given up more than Mr Donkey would ever achieve in his life. I could have said all this and much more to this silly ass, but now the time had come for silence. Goodbye to your patter, Mr Donkey. You won't get me into any kind of action, not even replying, I said silently in my mind.

Mr Donkey stopped running for a moment. Was he a thought-reader? Or, was he merely thinking what to say next? Whatever the reason, he was not allowed to muse much longer as there was a baying in the distance.

'Mate! Comrade! Partner! What are you standing still for? Aren't we on a great mission to show the world our worth? Aren't we to prove that donkeys are as great achievers and doers as any other species? There is so much to do, and you are taking a break? Have you completed your hundred laps of the farm? Have you completed your daily round of back jumping? Have you made the thousand somersaults? Have you . . .?'

Before the harangue could conclude, Mr Donkey was once again on the run. In a shamed voice he spoke out, 'I am sorry. I was distracted by a good-for-nothing bird who is sitting idle on a tree. I foolishly wanted to help him to become great achievers like us. I am conscious of my duties and responsibilities towards our farm, our land and our race. I am more than eager to contribute my share of running, jumping, leaping, cantering, and even galloping. Let the world see that we donkeys are not mere donkeys, but more than donkeys!'

Mr Hans whispered, 'If you do not want to keep jumping and galloping to prove a point, then come away.' I required no persuasion.

The Land of Shadow Chasers

'Could you reach your shadow Ms A?'

'No Ms B, I am still struggling. But for how long will it elude me? I am going to catch up with it sooner or later. And what about you, my friend? Have you succeeded?'

'I am in the same boat as everybody else in our land – struggling. But as you rightly pointed out, I will catch up with it soon.'

The people who were conversing in this way, were fair complexioned with a rosy tinge on their cheeks. They looked gentle and handsome, but had a touch of pathos about them; not as bad as the Leaktons, but on the way there. Something must be on their minds, I thought. Not being very sure, I asked Hans about them.

'We are in the land of shadow chasers. Here the sun rises for a very short time. During this time these people see their shadow, and want to reach it by incessant walking and jumping. Naturally they fail in their attempts, and then spend the long dark hours cursing their fate and crying over their failure.'

'What a place to be in!' I whispered back to Hans.

'Ms A,' said the pretty Ms B, 'I have heard from my parents and grandparents that those who succeed in catching their shadows, become immortal. My family has been making efforts to achieve this rare distinction for generations, but we have failed. I have examined many theories, and read many books including the famous *Possible Ways of Catching One's Shadow*, but nothing seems to work. Have you come across something new?'

'Friend, I read somewhere that if one sat down, one could catch one's shadow. But, the act is so demeaning and undignified that we should not even dream of doing it.'

'True. We have to consider our pride. I also read somewhere that if we walked facing the sun, then the shadow would follow us. Just the thought is horrible.'

'You are being polite, dear. It is worse than horrible. What about our complexion? We would lose that forever if the sunlight caught our face.'

'Right you are, m'am. In the meanwhile, let us not give up the quest. Today or tomorrow the shadows' luck would run out – they may even get tired of running and decide to stop. And then . . .!'

There was a look of intense expectation in the eyes of the speaker. You deluded people, I thought. Neither will the shadows stop running away from you, nor will the day come when you catch it.

'Mr Hans, who are these people? Gurus of ignorance?' I whispered.

'No. They are potential achievers. Only they have neither the submissiveness of Mr Donkey, nor the will to struggle like Mr Ambiger. They only know the goal, and want to achieve it without paying the price.'

'How long will they continue like this?'

'Forever and ever. Their offspring will keep carrying the baton handed over to them.'

'Sir, I have had enough. Let us leave quietly, else I might also want to chase shadows all my life.' It was only much later I realised that I myself had been chasing shadows, mirages and phantoms all my life.

The Garden of Weeds

'Why don't they just burn the weeds to get rid of the seeds?'

'That is the question, Tiya.'

This was what I asked Hans after we had fled from the land that I am just about to describe. I had never seen such a lush green land before – but the greenery came from nothing but weeds. We could see a large number of people working on plots of land, with a terrible looking demon shouting orders at them and cracking a whip.

'You rubber dolls! Can't your hands move? Work faster, or else . . . Do I pay you for your laziness?' the demon hollered. He cracked his whip on the nearest worker and everyone cried out in pain and fear. I was completely mystified by the sight.

'Huzoor, we are working very fast, as you may see yourself. But even before we have uprooted a bunch of these weeds, their seeds fall on the ground and shoot up as fresh plants. It is all seeds and weeds, sir,' said a worker.

'Yes, yes. I have heard that many times in the past. I don't want words – I want action. Perform or perish.' There was another crack of the whip and everyone cried out in collective pain. It seemed that all the workers were connected with each other, so the pain of one caused equal pain to the others. Unfortunately, they were helpless in getting rid of their own pain or that of others. I felt enveloped in sadness.

There was another crack of the whip and more cries rent the air.

'Huzoor, you are our lord and master; we have sold our souls to you. Have mercy on us, and do not hit us. We are working at your farm on empty bellies. We do not have enough food nor enough time to eat . . .' said another tortured worker.

'Stop! Stop!' shouted the demon. 'Your words smell of revolution! Wait till I teach you how to talk less and work more. The change you require will come from my whip on your backs.'

There were sounds of furious slashing, followed by pathetic cries and helpless groans.

A third worker cried out, 'Sir, do not hit us. The faster we work, the faster the weeds grow. I think that if we slow down, the weeds will also grow more slowly, and your garden would be rid of them. That is the only way to get freedom for the garden and for ourselves.'

'What an excellent excuse for working less!' retorted the demon. 'Wait! My whip will teach you to think more clearly. Here I come!'

Cries and more cries followed.

I quaked with fear. If I opened my mouth, would I also become a slave to this demon? I dashed away faster from that land than I had from any other place. Once safely out, I asked Hans about the mystery.

'The demon captures these innocent labourers by promising them that once their allotted patch of land is cleared of weeds, he will give them a purse of gold. But till it isn't cleared, the person shall be under his control. These needy souls fall for this trap and keep working like slaves. Their greed, hope and fear makes them work faster and in the process, the demon gets richer,' Hans explained.

'But how is that?' I asked. 'Weeds are weeds, aren't they?'

'The demon is not interested in getting his garden cleared. These weeds have healing properties, and when uprooted, they give rise to more and more weeds. The demon sells them and makes a fortune out of the free labour of his slaves.'

'Why don't these slaves just burn the weeds to get rid of the seeds?' I asked in exasperation.

'That is the million seed question, Tiya,' said Hans. They partly don't understand, and partly don't have the courage to do it. Words give birth to words, and action gives birth to action – the cycle continues.'

Hans was correct. I remembered how at the banyan, a quarrel among the birds caused more words to erupt, and how a fight between any two birds soon engulfed all. But despite Hans' words, I felt sad.

There were many more encounters and adventures, but to cut a long story short, I will move over to the last and major one.

The Wise Ones

Now the presence of Hans was with me more intensely than the visible presence of any others had ever been. My journeys with him had a different flavour. As promised, I had become a mute witness to whatever was happening all around. I used to ask Hans the occasional question in order to understand something. I wondered if others could also hear his formless voice – probably not. Anyone watching me talk to thin air would have doubted my sanity.

'Come, enter this hall with me. Just listen and watch – no comments, right?' said Hans to me.

'Right, sir,' I replied.

We were in a magnificent hall, in the centre of which was a table with heaps of food. Being essentially a fruit bird, I was not interested in the dainties, but there was something about it that

attracted my attention. I felt as if the heap held the key to something strange and mysterious. Seated around the table were seven important looking creatures whose faces resembled crows. And like the crows, they looked smart and artful. The light of intelligence shone in their eyes, but the simplicity associated with deep knowledge, was missing from their expression.

There was no way I could introduce myself to these seven, but in my mind I decided to call them Genone, Gentwo, etc. These Gens were distinguishable by cloaks of different colours. A couple of them had also tried to look important by putting on a wig, one had shaved his head, and the rest had put on silly looking top hats. Whatever they were waiting for, had to be quite important and solemn. They watched the heaps of untouched food before them.

Genone said: 'Glory unto the Lord. Brains In Arms! As usual we meet over dinner for our narration. The same rule holds – the greatest among us will be our President, will say grace and cut the cake. May we each begin by explaining what we have achieved, and then let us all decide whose achievement has been the greatest. We are humble servants of the Lord, and owe all that we have to Him. Naturally no one amongst us likes to boast of what he has done, but in the interest of the universe, each one will have to speak out.'

I wanted to cry out, 'Pompous ass!' but remembered Hans' warning and kept quiet. My stomach started swelling with unspoken words.

Gentwo began: 'My achievements have made me humble. I feel shy, but the rules force me to talk. Our last meeting ended in strong disagreement. I am glad to say that I have worked out the mother of all mathematical equations. Starting from the rate of the fall of a sparrow, it can calculate and predict God's every will, including your sneezes.'

'Wah wah!' the other Gens said in a chorus.

My feathers began itching to find out a little more. I wanted to ask him when I would be able to reach the banyan, but I restrained myself.

Said Genthree: 'We must congratulate Lord X for his achievement. Personally I bow low before him. I do not wish to be proud, but I must say that I have found out the how, why and when of the universe to the most minute details.'

Everyone was barking out 'Wahs!' I wondered how so much sound could come out of those narrow beaks.

Genfour then said: 'I must congratulate you Lord Y. But, without being immodest, I wish to add that I have found out the chemical that is the mother of all chemicals. It can create life, and destroy life. This finding of mine contradicts you two. There are no blind laws to govern the universe, nor is there any will of God to rule it. God is not needed for creation or destruction – it is all free will, free effort and freedom.'

My head was buzzing. Gentwo was on his feet at once: 'Mr President! I would appreciate if Lord Z confined himself to the impersonal. Those who deal in material matters must not comment on God. What would happen if the chemical of Lord Z is used by a person with the intent of creation and also destruction of the same object? Will that be living death, or deadly living?'

'MAAAAAAD!' I shrieked in complete frustration. The shriek echoed across the hall and had all eyes turned towards me – but thinking that I was a mere parrot having a nightmarish dream, they turned back to their discussion.

There was no sound from Hans. I knew that he was there, and must have given one of those invisible smiles. I was feeling guilty, so I did not interfere further.

The noise from the wise ones grew from a discordant din to a detonating crescendo, their verbal abilities matching their vocal prowess. It was complete mayhem now and instead of presenting their views, they had descended to simply ridiculing each other.

Suddenly there was banging of the gavel and everyone fell silent.

Genone said: 'It was nice to hear your views Brains In Arms. Let us agree to disagree, as we have always done in the past. The food stays untouched, as is the custom. You may take a glass of water if it pleases you, and then depart.'

We left the hall and I asked Hans in serious earnestness, 'Sir, what was the purpose of this visit of ours?'

'Didn't you see your reflection in any one of them?' Hans asked in mock surprise.

I let the comment pass, and asked, 'Sir, are the so-called wise ones really so dumb? Or do they pose like this to reach something higher?'

'What else will they do, Tiya? The ordinary must pose to look extraordinary – to feel and appear important is the biggest thrill. That is what makes life go on.'

' But sir . . . this is going too far, isn't it? Can't you do something to save these unfortunate ones?

They seem so badly locked up in their insane dreams!'

'I am for all, Tiya. Some don't allow my presence, some drive me away, some ignore my efforts, and worse still, some wish to destroy me by making an about turn.'

I wondered what he meant by that.

Part IV

The Land of Eternity

I was overwhelmed by the last words of Hans. After a long flight in silence, I dared to speak.

'Sir, Hans.'

'Yes Tiya?'

'Don't you suffer from emotions? Don't you ever get a high or a low? How do you keep so calm?'

'I neither enjoy, nor suffer. I just watch.'

'Who are you really? What is your true identity?'

'Know yourself, and you will know everything else.'

I knew very well who I was – Tiya the parrot. What else was I to know about myself? Instead, I started thinking more and more about Hans and his identity. He was invisible, but always by my side.

Was he a part of me? But that was not possible. How could a part of me stay outside me?

The questions and counter questions kept me occupied completely, when I was lifted out of this mental ocean by Hans' words.

'How would it be if you were to retrace your steps?'

There is a time for joking and a time to be serious. If Hans was joking, then it was the wrong time; and if he was serious, then it really sounded like a joke to me. To convey my disapproval, I merely lifted my left wing and gave it a shake to brush away some imaginary dirt.

Seeing that there was no reaction, I broke out in a more serious tone, 'Don't frighten me, sir! I start sweating when I look back at my adventures. The bad ones were frightening, and the good ones ensnared me. It is a wonder that beings survive here at all.'

No, Hans had not intended to make fun of me. His words now sounded as serious as his voice.

'You aren't wrong. People do not really survive here, they only think that they survive – more dead than alive.'

'I don't know how I managed to come out of those lands,' I said. 'Probably some power was protecting and guiding me all along. But I have a question, sir. Is there any way out for a chance visitor?'

'There is only one way out,' said Hans. 'One has to face the situation, but one also has to learn not to take a plunge. The unending journey takes one from situation to situation. One cries and smiles, desires something more, reaches new inevitabilities, meets new creatures, and the journey continues. This also means that there is nothing called chance. Only those events for which you are fit, come to you. In turn they take you to places for which you are fit. You won't even notice something for which you were not meant – good or bad.'

'Hmm.'

We birds don't absorb sound, we create it. My adventures had changed this trait of mine over these last few days, and I was slowly outgrowing my past. My experiences had given me enough depth to listen to Hans in silence and with patience. I did not yet fully understand all that he said, but I also did not run away from his words, nor did I ridicule them as I used to previously.

My silence egged him on.

'Events come of their own – although one wrongly thinks that these can be shaped or directed by individuals. What you can really control is your reactions to them. The more neutral you stay to them, the better the chance of your coming out successfully. Dislike for a thing is as bad as forming a liking for it; both are equally capable of binding you down.'

What could I say to these words that were far above my understanding! I merely reacted with a 'Hmm'. Hans also became silent. I was sitting on the branch of a stunted tree and was looking at a vast stretch of land that was dotted with small shrubs. Even the blades of grass seemed shorter than usual. Animals and birds were not to be seen anywhere.

The soothing presence of Hans was a great comfort. I was glad that he was my guide and benefactor. I was also happy because it saved me from making decisions. What was happening? Had I started growing humble? Once Mr Owl had scolded me and said, that to become great one had to be humble. I had also heard Mr Woodpecker say, that one felt great in the presence of the great. It must be the presence of Hans, which was impacting me silently.

That is when I heard him say, 'Tiya, you are now entering an unusual land.'

My mind had been meandering in useless thought. Without my guide, I could have spent my whole life thinking wild, planning big, and achieving nothing. However, there was nothing new in what Hans had just said. Unusual land! What else was I doing other than flying to unusual lands since the day I had left the banyan, I thought.

Banyan! My heart missed a beat. I longed for my friends whom I had nearly forgotten in the race of events. I had to tell Hans what my mind really desired.

'Sir, help me to go back to my good old banyan,' I said softly.

'That is what I am trying to do, Tiya. You will now have to cross this land that we have entered and fly over the mountains that guard it. However, keep in mind that in this mysterious land, the paths intertwine in such a way that even without your realising it, you may go back to the places that you have already visited. And keep in mind that this time, it will be difficult for you to come out so easily. Only by making the right effort can you go back to your banyan tree. The mountains are high, and the land is tricky – be careful. I can be of no use to you now, you are on your own.'

Whoops! I felt so happy. Banyan! At long last I would be reaching there soon. I felt like spinning in mid-air. Hurrah! No more destructive experiences for me. Yeah!

I looked down. The land looked flat, which meant that not much danger lay ahead. One short flight, and I would be back home. Home, dear home!

I didn't wait for Hans to say a further word. The joy in my heart made my body lighter and my mind clear – like a transparent balloon on a buoyant ride. With a smile, I made a diagonal flight – forward and upward.

To my horror I found myself flying forward but downward! The very next moment I was lying on the ground, face down – unable to fly. Feeling more silly than I had ever felt before, I tried my wings – but they seemed utterly incapable of lifting me up.

'Learn to listen, my young hero. When you are too eager, your troubles get bigger.'

Only my respect for Hans kept my lips sealed. 'Tell me Tiya, is the banyan everything to you? Can't you think of something more? Does life begin and end with the tree?' he continued.

Here I was burning with indignation at my great fall, and here was Hans, talking philosophy in his usual way.

'Sir, after getting to know you, I feel hesitant to bare my mind before you. I assure you that I have the highest respect and admiration for you, but I also consider you and your words quite weird at times. What do you mean by your question, sir? Is there anything beyond the good old banyan? Is there anything beyond life and living? Is there anything beyond tears and smiles?'

'Who knows? There might be.'

What an odd reply.

The way Hans answered my questions was distinctively odd. Sometimes his answers came as free flowing and transparent as a hill stream, and at other times they were as opaque and hard as old blocks of ice. But this did not matter with me anymore. I had grown to love him much beyond a normal bird's love. I didn't know who he was, but I felt that without him I had no existence. By now I also knew that he would always be there with me in my life, death, success, failure, sorrow and joy. Did his identity matter anymore? I liked him the way he was – at least, as long as he was with me. That is why I tolerated whatever he uttered.

I would have continued floating in the undertow of this mental whirlpool when I heard, 'You are at your journey's end, Tiya. Get up and start. You only have to cross this land and fly beyond the mountains. The rest will follow automatically.'

'I feel weak, sir. Will it be possible for me to do what you ask?' I was alluding to my inability to fly.

'Yes Tiya, you can, and you will. Just know a few things. This unusual land has no name, so you may as well call it the land of eternity. Like a maze, it is easy to enter it, but nearly impossible to get out. Many have entered and returned to the same old lands of adventure. Many are still wandering aimlessly here. The vicious power of the place pulls everything down and keeps one tied to oneself. The only way to get out is to apply one's right mind and make the maximum effort. So, apply what you have learnt during your journey. I can't be of any use to you here. Now you are on your own.'

Another of his riddles, I thought. But it was not so. Instead of his presence, I was now surrounded by his absence. He was really gone and I felt lonely. But my journey had to be completed. There would be enough time for tears – and for smiles too. Emotions could not be the speed breakers on the road of responsibility.

I applied myself to my task and tested my wings. They seemed complete and whole. I tested my legs by walking – it was difficult, but not impossible. I simply needed to bridge my captivity and freedom by walking. Everything now depended on me. A tremendous urgency overcame me – after knowing that the key to freedom lay ahead of me, I wanted to hurry.

Heavy steps slowed down my speed. The gravity of the place made me heavier and seemed to suck away my energy. It would be difficult to continue without proper nourishment, I thought. But where would I get it?

Suddenly my eyes caught sight of a pile of fruits and nuts not far away. I advanced towards it with measured steps, but I felt that something was not very right. I was not very sure if I was supposed to take what lay before me. We birds normally eat what is on a tree or fallen down. But here the fruits were arranged in a heap and probably someone owned them.

My mind now hovered around one of Mr Woodpecker's famous sayings: 'Touch not what is not yours.' At our banyan, the daily evening news used to be about some foolish bird who had been trapped that day. The pigeons were the worst lot. Everyday a few of them used to get caught, simply because they were too greedy and pounced upon any loose grain that met their eyes. I steeled myself and stayed away from the nuts and fruits that had seemed to appear magically before me. Without my knowing it, I had conquered the first real temptation of my life – the pile vanished as magically as it had appeared.

I was fed up with my adventures much before I had reached this land of eternity. The seed of discontentment in my mind had been watered by disillusionment, and now it had grown into a tree that bore the fruit of detachment. I was completely detached and only wanted to get out of the place at any cost. My feathers felt as if they were on fire that needed putting out immediately. I wanted my freedom first – gains and losses could be calculated later.

I applied my mind to the present – my freedom had to be attained through detachment and hard work. Instead of flying, I would have to walk for a while. So I decided that I would do that, come what may.

I had cursed those revolutionary birds, but now I felt thankful to them. It was from them that I had learnt how to walk. I had cursed my fate when I was forced to endure my stay there, but it was only the experience and power gained during that suffering, which now made me capable of gaining my freedom. No experience is meaningless in life, I thought. I was lost in my thoughts when I saw some birds walking like me at a distance. A closer look showed that they were the very birds I had been thinking about – what a wonderful coincidence!

'Hello!' I cried out.

The birds just looked at me with an amused smile.

'How is the Big Bird? Still terrorising you folks?'

The frightened look on their faces made me look around. It was the Big Bird himself. In person – not far from where I was! But I was not afraid anymore. Since I was not in his land, I had no reason to be scared.

Knowing that the other birds would not approach me because of the Big Bird, I continued walking – and thinking. A lonely traveller has only thoughts for company. One thought led to another, and another. I was soon swamped by the memories of my recent past, which came back to me in a quick sequence. I remembered the good, the bad, and the neutral, with a certain tenderness. My eyes were fixed to the ground, but my mind was reaching out everywhere.

I raised my vision to find my bearings and the wonder of wonders met my eyes. Everyone I had interacted with in the past, was present in front of me. Had they escaped from their lands and succeeded in reaching the last milepost? Was I in some way responsible for their release? I felt very happy for them – and for myself.

There were a multitude of birds and creatures all around me. They were of all kinds – colourful, dull, singers, talkers, flyers, walkers, riders, hoppers . . .There were the razor-fingered Fays with their enchanting smiles; the Zarys spitting furiously all around; the wailing Leaktons; and many more . . . I had not even seen some of the creatures who were now in front of me – I had seen some only from a distance. There were some whom I had imagined, some who had appeared to me in pleasant dreams, and some in nightmares. I had liked some, and disliked others. The noble and the wicked were mingled together. Turn in whichever direction I might, they were present everywhere.

And strangely, the intensity of their feelings for me was much more than in the past. I could see it in their eyes.

'Tiya, move on,' a part of my mind warned me. Another part of it drew me closer to this milling crowd. A loud babble enveloped the air.

'My dear, are you really annoyed with me? You left in such a hurry. I never meant you any harm.'

'You nut-brained-nut-cracker! If only my hands were free, I would have freed your nut forever.'

'This time you won't escape my stew pot. I have brought onions to make it taste better.' The fisherman advanced towards me and I cowered.

'Ha, ha! Our feathery hero! Here you are at last. Just look around. How many of us are here to hear your jokes and see you spin.'

'Come, we will teach you to sum up two twos, three threes, four fours . . .'

'Forget the fools and focus on . . .'

'. . . five fives, six sixes . . .'

'. . . infinity.'

'Cutie, come dear. I will make you . . .'

'Catch him, catch him!'

'. . . happy.'

The voices went on and on, and my emotions surged up and down with them. I was happy, sad, afraid, angry, loving, and jealous – all in quick succession. Each emotion was much stronger than what I had felt in the past. My mind raced, whirled and spun.

Puzzled beyond power, I waited to calm myself down. Slowly, the intensity within me diminished, and surprisingly, the crowd outside started to decrease. Finally very few were left, but they showed an increased intensity.

I wanted to escape, but needed the help of Hans. Where was he? Why was he always absent when his presence was badly needed?

But, no – here he was. Just by my side. Hans the swan. Dazzling in his beauty. Oh, what a fool I had been!

'How beautiful and bright you are, Hans. Your splendour even outshines the sun!'

'True.'

'I wish to be with you and you alone for the rest of my life. What a stupid life I have been living!'

'True.'

'I have been such a fool – even been so obnoxious with you.'

'True.'

'I won't ever leave you again. Nor will you leave me, please.'

'True.'

I relaxed now. All the other creatures were gone – like stars in the daytime. It was only me, Hans, and our company. Dear Hans – the meaning of my life. My joy.

This would have continued till eternity – that is what this land was meant for. But, something made me uneasy and I looked up. There was another Hans high up in the sky – huge and majestic, with its wings spanning the entire planet. Lighting up even the sun.

How could that be? Were there two Hans? One with me – and another covering the whole sky and much more? It just could not be possible. One had to be fake – an illusion.

'Hans, you are imaginary!'

'True.'

'I want to get away from you.'

'True.'

'But, I can't leave you!'

'True.'

'Please, please, go away. I want to find the real you.'

What was happening to me? What was real and what was unreal? What was true and what was fake? Who was Hans? Who was I? WhowasHanswhowasI? My mind froze. Layer after layer was bared before my mind's eyes. I was numb and my mind had gone silent. Nothing existed around me – only space and more space . . .

As if in a dream, my past came rushing back at me. Now I confronted my true nature and my real home.

My past seemed utterly ridiculous to me, as I realised that all my pain and suffering had been brought upon me by myself. I alone was responsible for the bitter and sweet experiences of my life – the joys and miseries, smiles and tears, pleasure and pain. They were all like the waves of the mighty ocean – unable to touch the depths. These experiences came and went without touching the real me. They were like teachers to whom one went to learn, but not to settle down with – essential, but not permanent.

It was fortunate that I was not aware of what I had learnt during the actual time of my adventures; that would have left the game incomplete and inconclusive. It could have also made my agony unbearable. I now realised the truth of 'ignorance is bliss', and that it is ignorance that makes life go on smoothly. Without it, either life would not continue, or it would be too painful to live. That is when I also realised that 'knowledge without accomplishment is pain'. I learnt about the real me in those moments of revelation and I will tell you about it yet.

My real home is far, far away – beyond the white clouds, the blue sky, and the bright stars. Anyone can belong to that place, and that is the way one becomes special. In that place, you can go anywhere on a mere wish, you can get any form of nourishment without any effort, and you can read any mind like an open book. There is nothing that is secret or valuable in that land, be they places, objects or minds. There, it is eat at will, rest at will, play at will, travel at will, have fun at will. There are no paths or goals. There is neither any hurry, nor stress. It is the land of plenty and peace; it is the land of lands – 'our land'.

Hans was right. I was much more than a parrot.

I had been bored with the listless life that I was leading in our land. I knew every nook and cranny, every inhabitant – their minds and games. Nothing spectacular happened there, nor was anything expected to happen. Only the new arrivals, and that too far and few between, brought some variety. A misleading elder had once told me that the more exciting folks went to the other land because of the funny life that they had led in the past. Also, the variety of that other place attracted many more experimental minds than our land could ever attract. Whatever the reasons, we led a monotonous life.

If ever any newcomers arrived, we youngsters would surround them to hear their spellbinding stories. But the exciting experiences of these folks used to make me feel more lonely and lost. I felt surprised at the excitement the new ones displayed on reaching our land. What was ordinary and natural for me was extraordinary for them. However, they would lose their sheen in a few days and the more mature among us never paid any attention to them or their words.

I now realise why I had started pining for adventures. Broken strands of sentences like, 'fun, sin, horror, greed' used to hang like cobwebs in my otherwise clean mind. I wondered about the meaning of these terms and why we did not experience these in our land. Was there more to the existence than I knew? I felt that I had to experiment in order to become complete. I knew that I would have to leave this place and seek what others had in their lands.

My strong desire to experience life had created a hollowness inside me.

You know the rest.

Today I wonder how many like me must be wandering all over the world.

The only thing that mattered now was my freedom from the double captivity. I looked around. All the creatures had gone. Only Hans remained – below and above.

'Please, Hans. Please go away if you are not real,' I moaned.

'I cannot. You created me – placed me here. I cannot go away.'

'Help me, Hans. Help me. Tell me how to get out of this field of influence?'

'Find the way.'

I felt as if the Hans of the sky was tipping his wings and winking his eyes to me. Was it my imagination? Or was it a sign that he wanted me above? I felt insane with eagerness to get out. My humour, wisecracks, intelligence, anger, and sense of power had vanished. There was only one thing left in me – the desire to fly away to Hans above. I tried to blank out my mind from everything else and gave my legs a big push. I rose, and then fell, feeling deeply embarrassed. Some of the phantoms of my past appeared in front of me and laughed

cruelly at my plight. But I had learnt my lessons
– no more repartees or angry words at their jibes.
I knew the dreadful consequences. These creatures
appeared only when I thought of them.

I tried to fly again with utmost concentration,
but I failed once more. Would I ever succeed, I
despaired. My life, my happiness, my freedom
– everything now depended on my effort. I
remembered the words of Hans saying that I could
achieve much more than what I thought I could. I
felt inspired and desperate to struggle once again,
but my past was not willing to give me a break.

Hans above – in you lies my freedom.

Hans below – you are the last barrier between
me and my freedom. You are my creation and also
my cage. I will have to crush you for my freedom.
But how could I destroy my own creation! It
seemed utterly painful to me. To break the cage,
smash my chains, and free myself, I would have to
destroy my Hans.

I once again concentrated on my single-
minded desire to be free. One big push towards
Hans in the sky. All had gone blank inside me.
That is what I remember. After that nothing
remained . . . the earth seemed to tremble. The
crash that followed was enough to shake the skies

and unleash thunder and lightning. Everything of this universe seemed to melt into one.

I thought I heard Nature heave a sigh.

It's difficult for me to describe what happened or remained after that.

Only the story continues.

I flew back to my banyan. Free – externally and internally. My old friends greeted me noisily.

'Ha, ha, ha. Welcome back, our hero.'

'How did the wide world treat you Tiya? Could you get good nuts and fruits?'

'Did you miss us Tiya? You look changed.'

I gave an indulgent smile. They would not understand what I had to say – it was meaningless to them.

'What a combination! Red on green. Ha, ha, ha. Green welcomes and red stops. One cannot decide whether to go near him or not! Ha, ha, ha!'

In the past I used to get angry at such personal remarks. Now I was indifferent. The words of the birds neither amused me, nor annoyed me. To make my intentions clear, I remained silent. One of my old friends came to my aid. 'Leave him alone. He is not what he was. Leave him alone.' I felt grateful.

'A lot has happened since you left, Tiya,' he said. 'I will tell you all the gossip as soon as you are ready.'

'Later,' I said.

'What is wrong with you?' he asked in a puzzled voice. 'Till the other day you were the soul of our laughter, and today you seem so indifferent.'

'No. No. Carry on with your fun. One less won't make a difference, will it?' I said.

My friend agreed with me and hopped on to another branch to find a more agreeable listener.

I watched.

Epilogue

I have achieved much more than I had ever imagined I could as Tiya, and I am indeed much more than what I had thought I was. In fact no one in this universe is ordinary. Most do not know this – a few feel it within themselves – but a majority do not care.

The story may have touched you. Every time you look at a shooting star you may think it to be a foolish and adventurous soul. Every time you see a bird, you may think of a lost soul fooling around. And, every time you see a parrot with a red ring around its neck, you may think it is me. You may wonder if it's Tiya, watching your inexperience through his experiences.

In fact, you may very well be correct.

My adventures are over. I do not live at the banyan anymore; even the banyan was only a part of my adventures. Now I know who I am – I know my real home.

I am waiting for my return. I have to wait for

a while – till the season of soft mist arrives. Then I will board one of those white autumn clouds and be gone forever. I will be united with my real nature, my real home, and my real friends. But until I am near you, I must narrate my adventures to as many listeners as I can find – and quickly. My story told and retold, may drive them to attain their uniqueness; to attain the apparently unattainable.

Whenever you see a parrot, remember me and my unusual story.